BLINDFOLD

Blindfold

Sophie Danson

First published in 1997
by HEADLINE BOOK PUBLISHING

A HEADLINE LIAISON paperback

10 9 8 7 6 5 4 3 2 1

ISBN 0 7472 5583 0

Typeset by CBS, Felixstowe, Suffolk

Printed and bound in Great Britain by
Mackays of Chatham plc, Chatham, Kent

HEADLINE BOOK PUBLISHING
A division of Hodder Headline PLC
338 Euston Road
London NW1 3BH

Blindfold

Chapter 1

Alexa de Maas shifted in her seat and squinted out of the carriage window, shading her eyes against the watery December sunshine. There was a certain something about Doncaster railway station. An ambience. It was hard to define, but whatever it was, it wasn't glamour.

People in scarves and bobble-hats scuttled about on the platform, voices occasionally raised to curse a dropped suitcase or a snivelling child. It seemed as if everyone in the world wanted to cram onto the same train, in their race to get to the other end of the country before New Year's Eve.

'Bye Kev, bye Tracey, be good for Granny. And wipe that chocolate off your mouth.'

'The train now standing at Platform Four is the delayed 07.17 from Plymouth to Newcastle . . .'

'Where's the other bag? Tim, what've you done with the other bag, it's got the turkey sandwiches in it.'

'Just one more goodbye kiss, darling. If I don't get off the train right now, it'll go with me still on it.'

To judge from the girl's expression, she wouldn't have minded if it did, thought Alexa. The train doors slammed shut and Alexa turned back to her magazine, gladder than ever that she'd persuaded the Agency to pay the extra and let her travel first class.

As she'd told her boss, Damian, this was a business trip and it wouldn't do the Agency's image any favours if she turned up at the conference looking – and feeling – like a wrung-out J-cloth.

Kicking off her shoes, she stretched out her legs and wiggled her smarting toes. With fresh coffee and a chocolate-chip cookie for company, *Cosmo* and a G & T for dessert, she settled down to some well-earned self-indulgence.

The sudden brr-brr of her mobile phone cut through the silence and she rummaged irritably in her bag, aware of disapproving eyes glaring at her over laptop PCs.

'Yes?'

'Alexa. It's me.'

'Piet!' She huddled into the angle of the seat and the window, crossing her smooth-stockinged legs. 'I can't talk now, I'm on the train.'

'So don't talk, just listen. I'm missing you.'

'Me too, but . . .'

'You were gone when I woke up.' The voice was sweetly, coaxingly accusing.

'I didn't want to wake you.' She recalled how she'd tiptoed around in the semi-darkness, closing the bedroom door behind her with nothing more than a soft click.

'You should have. I was dreaming about fucking you.'

'Piet!' Colouring slightly, Alexa cupped her hand round the phone, half-convinced that everyone in the carriage could hear what her husband was saying.

2

'We could have acted out my dream,' Piet went on.'Shall I tell you what we were doing?'

'Now's not the time for this, Piet, I'm supposed to be working, remember . . . ?'

Piet made a chuckling noise, low in his throat. His laughter was one of the things that had attracted Alexa to him; he had a supremely dirty laugh which made your thoughts stray to forbidden sex the moment you first looked into those catlike, hazel-gold eyes.

'Relax. Just sit back and listen. You know what a vivid imagination I have . . .'

Naturally she could have switched off the phone and stopped him right there, but as usual curiosity got the better of her. Besides, Piet's voice caressed and seduced like a gigolo's. As she closed her eyes and pressed the receiver to her ear, she could almost believe he was sitting right beside her, whispering his desire as his fingers walked slowly and tantalisingly over her skin.

'I'm too hot to wait any longer, you know that, don't you?' whispered Piet, his cultured voice faintly and exotically accented. 'Hotter than hot.'

'You always were too impatient for your own good,' smiled Alexa, remembering the first time they'd made love; the animal urgency of their passion as they'd tumbled through the door of Piet's then office and turned the key in the lock. 'Hold all calls, we definitely don't want to be disturbed,' he'd told his secretary, and she'd just smiled and nodded like this kind of thing happened all the time in the world of international banking. And perhaps it did . . .

3

'I won't take you to the bedroom,' Piet continued. 'I think I'll just have you over the kitchen table. Would you enjoy that, Alexa? It's OK, you don't have to say, I *know* you would . . .'

She didn't speak, but giggled nervously, her face turned resolutely away from the nearest passenger, a hatchet-faced business type in an undertaker's black suit.

'You're straight out of the bath, all you're wearing is that red Chinese silk robe – you remember the one? I brought it back for you from Shanghai.'

'Of course I remember.'

And I recall what we did the very first time I wore it, she added silently, smiling to herself. On the landing carpet, with the Axminster rubbing friction burns into the small of my back. That poor silk robe had to go straight off to the dry cleaners the very next day.

'You're standing in the doorway of the kitchen, asking me if I'm hungry. And the robe's falling open at the front, I can almost see your nipples. Hungry? Do you realise what you're saying? And then you ask me, "What do you want for breakfast?" I want *you* for breakfast, Alexa. Lightly squeezed, freshly peeled, au naturel . . .'

Alexa's right hand was resting lightly on her thigh. Eyes closed against the flickering sunlight, she could almost imagine it was Piet's hand, and the gentle rocking motion of the carriage the rhythm of his breathing.

'If you don't stop this now, Piet, I'm going to ring off.'

'If you do, I'll call straight back.'

'Then I'll switch the phone off.'

'No you won't. And you won't cut me off, because you

4

want to know what happens next.' He teased her with a kind of gentle insistence. 'Don't you?'

Alexa's thumb hovered over the off button for a couple of seconds, then relaxed. She reached for the plastic cup of coffee and took a sip.

'OK then, Piet. Why don't you tell me a bedtime story?' Her gaze flicked round the carriage. Other eyes met hers briefly, then darted away, denying that they had ever made contact or shown the slightest interest in what she was doing. Denying that they could possibly have overheard the word 'bedtime'. 'But you'd better make it a good one.'

'It's a good one, all right. You're laughing and wriggling as I lay you down on the kitchen table. There's butter in your hair, and marmalade and coffee all over your robe, the red satin's all soaked through. You'll have to take it off. And I'll have to lick you clean . . .'

'Ah, but will I let you?'

'You'd be mad not to. Nobody knows your pussy like I do. And just think how sensational it will feel when I take that aerosol cream out of the fridge and spray it between your thighs . . .'

'You wouldn't!'

'. . . little swirling patterns of cream all over the insides of your thighs and pretty rosettes inside your sex. You'll look just like an ice-cream sundae. Shall I sprinkle you with chocolate vermicelli and garnish you with a maraschino cherry? I promise I'll eat it all up . . .'

Alexa put her hand to her mouth to stifle a jittery laugh. There was a dull, throbbing ache between her thighs, as though in her imagination she could already feel Piet's adventurous tongue, hot and wriggling in an ocean of chilled whipped cream.

'You're a wicked boy, Piet de Maas.'

'Guilty.' He paused.'Where are you?'

'On the train, I told you.'

'I know that, but *where*?'

'I dunno. A few miles out of Doncaster, the middle of nowhere.'

'And wouldn't you rather be back home, seeing in the New Year with me?'

'You know I would.'

It was half true, thought Alexa, but only half. She did miss Piet, but then again this was her first major conference, her first big chance to represent SuccessWorks and get herself noticed. It meant a lot to her, she'd been looking forward to it for ages and Piet knew it.

'So why don't you just get off and take the next train back?'

'I can't!'

'Sure you can.'

'I'm not letting the Agency down, Piet, not for anything.'

'Not even for me?'

Alexa couldn't quite decide if the resentment in his voice was real or just play-acting.

'What's got into you, Piet? Is this emotional blackmail or something? All I'm doing is going to a conference for a few days . . .'

'Yeah. To spend New Year's Eve with about two dozen horny young advertising executives.'

'Don't give me that jealousy crap. You spend half your life away on business trips.'

'Sure I do, working twenty hours a day and doing deals in my sleep.'

'This is no different. This is work too.'

'If you say so.'

Alexa caught the eye of the black-suited businessman across the gangway. He was smirking. Suddenly she felt supremely irritated. If Piet could have his brilliant career as a banking consultant, she could have her one small moment of glory.

'Grow up, Piet, don't you trust me or something?'

'Sure I do. But . . .'

'But nothing. I'm going to this conference so you'll just have to trust me, won't you? The way I have to trust you.'

There was a short silence, then Piet laughed. That same, sexy, seductive laugh that never failed to touch Alexa in all the right places.

'Just one more thing.'

'What's that?'

'Don't do anything I wouldn't do.'

Boroughbridge Hall was no more than a ten-minute taxi ride from York station. In fact it was barely outside the city walls, but you'd never have known it was there at all if not for the brass plaque set into the high encircling wall.

The main building dated back to the eighteenth century, and was set in nicely-manicured grounds dotted with the occasional ancient oak or beech. Squirrels chased each other along the bare, frosty branches, their tails undulating like

7

feather boas. Dead leaves and twigs crunched underfoot as Alexa hauled her suitcase up the front steps and walked into the lobby.

Mirrors lined the hallway which led to the reception desk, reflecting multiple images of a young woman in a plum-coloured tailored suit with velvet trim, black Dior ballet pumps and matching gloves. Her reddish-brown hair, lightly highlighted with a paler golden brown, was shoulder-length, tied back from her oval face in a pony-tail which danced as she walked.

This doesn't suit me, thought Alexa in a moment of panic, glancing at her reflection and wishing she had worn the blue suit instead of the plum. The cold weather had left her face ghost-white and her pourpre velours lipstick and large dark eyes seemed too dramatic against her pale skin. Still, at least it was warm inside the lobby – and what a lobby! Her eyes travelled upwards, past oak panelling and ornate plaster mouldings, to polished candelabra and a domed glass ceiling, from which hung an enormous chandelier. Tacky, she thought. Tacky but in the nicest possible way, a quintessentially upper-class English way.

A girl in a leather skirt and chenille sweater emerged from behind a reception desk half-hidden in the shadows.

'Hi, I'm Rosie – can I help?'

Alexa set down her case.

'I hope so, I'm here for the conference: "Marketing your Message in the Media Age" . . . ?'

Rosie smiled, her face impish and impossibly young beneath short, black razor-cut hair. She consulted her clipboard.

'And you are . . . ?'

'Alexa de Maas. I'm a graphic designer with the SuccessWorks PR agency, in Cirencester.'

'Right, Ms de Maas, if you'd like to follow me. Registration is just through here, most of the delegates have already arrived. When you've collected your badge and registration pack, perhaps you'd like to join some of the others for coffee in the Garden Room?'

Alexa followed Rosie through into a small room lined from floor to ceiling with books, and smelling strongly of mildew and old leather. People of all shapes and sizes were milling about – waitresses in black dresses and white aprons, a tall, aristocratic-looking woman in a low-cut green dress which matched her eyes, a few media darlings in black Escada and Louis Vuitton snakeskin print, a very handsome oriental girl and three laddish young clones in grey suits, busily practising their communication skills by chatting up one of the receptionists. Not my type at all, mused Alexa with perhaps a tiny twinge of disappointment. Piet needn't have bothered being jealous after all.

'Name, please?' enquired one of the receptionists.

'De Maas. Alexa de Maas.'

'Here's your badge, Ms de Maas, if you'll just sign here. There's coffee in the Garden Room, and the introductory address will be after dinner, in the ballroom. Oh, and here's your room key, you're in 601 in the west wing. Take the second left, straight on, left again and the lift's on your right.'

Second left . . . and the lift's on your right. Alexa picked up her case and wandered off in what she thought was vaguely the right direction. But she'd obviously got something wrong, because the second left and the third right took her to a set of French windows which looked out onto an enclosed courtyard. And rather more than that . . .

Alexa nearly dropped her suitcase on her foot as she stared out into the small, rectangular courtyard with its withered honeysuckle, lichen-covered stone seats and sunken lily-pond, crazy-paved with half-melted ice. For there were two people in the courtyard, apparently neither knowing nor caring if anyone could see what they were doing.

The woman was in her late twenties, very blonde and athletically built in a Scandinavian kind of way, crop-haired and stylishly dressed in an unstructured suit of slate-grey silk which softened the lines of her slightly mannish body. Her head was thrown back, her skirt ruched up around her waist and her bare thighs wrapped around the waist of a tall, raven-haired man in a dark Armani suit.

Alexa took a step closer to the French windows, scarcely believing what she was seeing. Her breath misted the glass and she wiped it away, not wanting to miss a single second, totally transfixed by the silent, erotic tableau.

The man's back was up against the yellowish-grey stone wall, his sea-grey eyes open and fixed straight ahead of him, unblinking, unfocused and almost trance-like. His lips were open and his shoulders rose and fell with the quickening rhythm of his breathing as his hands cupped and gripped the woman's bare buttocks and danced her up and down.

As she rose and fell, the glistening, waxy-pink stalk of a dick emerged and disappeared, emerged and disappeared, lingering only long enough to tantalise before being hidden from sight once again.

Alexa felt a rush of adrenaline, a guilty tingle animating her whole body, as though she was a small child who'd seen something she wasn't supposed to, something she'd be punished for later. Guilty and excited, that was how she felt. But guilty of what? She had no reason to feel remotely guilty. Embarrassed was nearer the mark: she'd simply stumbled on a particularly uninhibited couple who'd probably be mortified if they knew they had an audience. Good manners dictated that she ought just to turn and walk away, but fascination kept her rooted to the spot, drinking in every move of those two bodies, moving so smoothly and yet so passionately together.

She couldn't hear their moans and sighs through the glass, but she knew the woman was coming; felt every shudder as her body grew suddenly rigid and her mouth opened wide. Then she fell forward, her head resting on the man's shoulder.

They remained like that for a few seconds, maybe longer. Later, Alexa could only recall the episode as though it had been a dream, in which real time had stood still. Then the woman slid to the ground and eased down her skirt, shaking out the creases. She and the man scarcely exchanged a glance as he zipped himself up, and they turned and began walking towards the French windows.

Alexa caught her breath. They'd seen her now, it was pointless turning tail. But what was she going to say or do? The doors opened and the man and woman stepped inside. Eyes met. Alexa felt the woman's gaze travel over her body, then pale lips curved into a smile.

'Hi. You here for the conference too?'

'I . . . yes.'

11

The woman exchanged looks with her sometime lover. He was handsome, thought Alexa; or at least, compelling in an unconventional, darkly sardonic kind of way. But his eyes scarcely seemed to notice her, and for no reason at all, she felt curiously resentful.

'I'll look forward to seeing you later, then,' said the blonde woman. Then she and the man walked silently away, parting company at the end of the corridor and disappearing in opposite directions, as though they'd been exchanging no more than a few comments about the weather.

Alexa remained standing on the same spot for several minutes, trying to banish the images from her mind. Images of a man and a woman, rutting unashamedly right before her eyes. And Alexa was certain now, certain that they'd known she was there, and had *wanted* her to watch. Maybe having her there had even turned them on. Alexa was mildly ashamed of the sweet ache between her thighs which made her long to clench and rub them together. It was as if by watching the two lovers she had shared in the act of coupling, and now they were linked in a weird trinity by a kind of erotic complicity.

All of which was nonsense, of course. She'd seen two oversexed conference delegates having an unwary 'quickie' when they thought no one was looking. People always had sexual adventures at conferences, it was just that they weren't normally quite so blatant.

Her gaze slipped downwards to the paving stones which surrounded the lily pond. There, lying on the frosty ground, were the blonde woman's panties: a flimsy knot of something pink and gauzy, fluttering in the cold breeze like a stranded butterfly. The only tangible reminder of what Alexa had just seen.

Boroughbridge Hall wasn't your average conference venue, there was no doubt about that. At first, Alexa told herself she was imagining it, but one fact kept coming back to her again and again until she couldn't deny it any longer. The whole place was imbued with an atmosphere of intense eroticism.

It was almost as if some mad scientist had invented the world's most potent aphrodisiac and let it loose in the water supply. Every time you turned the corner, you half-expected to catch sight of people screwing in the shrubbery – which actually wasn't too far from the truth. Alexa liked to think of herself as broad-minded, liberated even, but it was hard to know what to say when you walked into the sauna, found three naked women making love in the steam, and were invited to join in.

Not that she did, of course. She was here on business. SuccessWorks expected results, and there was work to do. Work meant attending boring talks on the future of public relations, schmoozing anyone who might turn out to be a useful contact, drinking more alcohol than any normal liver could stand, and attending an endless round of seminars, role-playing sessions and workshops.

The following morning, she checked the noticeboard for details of the day's events. Ten-fifteen, in the library, 'Powerplay and motivation, a behavioural reappraisal'; she'd be giving that one a miss. One forty-five, in the long gallery, 'Marketing new product lines'; that looked slightly more promising. But no, this was what she'd been looking for: nine-thirty, in the conservatory, 'Creative Communication' with Miranda Ross, Creative Director of the New York PR Agency, Big Ideas. Damian had particularly wanted her to go to that one. What was it he'd said? 'Look, listen, learn – then steal all her best ideas.'

After breakfast, she took her second cup of coffee into the conservatory, chose a Lloyd loom chair in the discreet shade of a date palm, and checked that her tiny tape-recorder was switched on – her shorthand was rusty and she didn't want to miss anything. The word was that Miranda Ross was dynamite in Dolce & Gabbana.

Six or seven other delegates were already there, their chairs drawn into a rough semicircle around a low central platform with a chair and a flipchart. No sign of the two exhibitionists she'd seen in the courtyard, or the woman in the green dress. In fact, Alexa quickly realised that she was the only woman here.

'Hi.' A hand touched her lightly on the arm and she started. 'I'm with Bradstock, Humphrey and Tait. How about you?'

She turned her head and found herself looking into a smooth-skinned face that looked scarcely old enough to shave, let alone work in one of the premier London advertising agencies.

'SuccessWorks.' She felt vaguely irritated by the puppy-dog smile and the fingers that lingered a little too long on her arm.

'This is my first conference.'

'Really?'

'I'm really looking forward to Ms Ross's seminar, they're

calling her the future of corporate communication, you know?'

'You don't say.' Alexa detached herself from the long, slender fingers and wished she'd sat somewhere else. But it was too late now, a fat man in corduroy trousers was easing his backside onto the last empty chair.

'Maybe we could meet up in the bar afterwards, and compare notes over a bottle of Chardonnay?'

Dream on, thought Alexa. I've known sexier Boy Scouts. Then she relented. After all, everybody had to go through the embarrassing kid stage – even Piet must have done, though it was hard to imagine him as anything less than sexually confident.

'Sorry.' She smiled, but not too encouragingly. 'I have this rule about never mixing business with pleasure. I'm sure you understand.'

Whether he did or not, Alexa didn't much care. She was just glad to be free of him. As she looked away, she caught sight of a face, reflected in the glass wall of the conservatory. The face of a man, dark-haired, pale-skinned and rather angular. The ghost of a mocking smile was playing about his lips and his eyes were fixed squarely on her.

The man she'd seen in the courtyard.

A weird frisson ran up her spine, making the hairs stand up on the back of her neck. Before, he'd studiously ignored her; but now there was an alarming intensity in those eyes, the way they just kept on looking at her, drawing her to them and holding her there as though they were revelling in their own power. Arrogant bastard, he was laughing at her.

Turning towards the stranger, whose chair was almost

hidden behind one of the iron pillars which held up the wrought iron frame of the conservatory, Alexa met his stare full-on. He didn't so much as blink. In the end it was Alexa who backed down, using the arrival of Miranda Ross as a welcome excuse to break eye-contact.

'Good morning everyone, I'm Miranda, sorry I'm late but I got an urgent call from a client.'

A waft of Calvin Klein's Obsession filled the sun-warmed air as Miranda Ross breezed in, the curves of her petite figure emphasised by spray-on black leather trousers and a red cashmere T-shirt. Her kitten-heeled snakeskin shoes tapped like impatient fingernails on the marble tiles, her whole body as full of latent energy as a coiled spring. She opened her briefcase and took out a sheaf of papers.

'Hand these out, would you? One per person, we'll be looking at them later. Now.' She sat down on the plain bentwood chair and crossed her thighs. Alexa was struck by the iridescent blue polish on her smooth oval nails, which clashed shamelessly with the red and black clothes and the hennaed orange-red of her spiral-curled hair. 'Let's start getting to know each other.'

She turned her head very slowly from left to right, taking in the semi-circle of chairs and their occupants.

'OK, so I'm Miranda. But who are you?' She pointed a thin, blue-tipped finger at a man in trendy gold-rimmed glasses.

'Me? I'm Tony,' he said with an ingratiating smile. 'Tony Peterson, from Peterson Ronay.'

Miranda shrugged, her cheeks dimpling slightly as she pursed her lips.

'So that's your name, but who *are* you, Tony?'

'Sorry?'

'I mean, what really makes you tick?' As Tony didn't reply, she went on. 'OK, so let me explain. I'm Miranda, I live in New York City. I like chocolate macadamia nuts and if I don't have at least six orgasms a day I get really unpleasant to live with.' Her eyes returned to Tony. 'So how about you, Tony? You like to screw?'

To Alexa's amusement, Tony coloured up.

'Well, you know. I mean, doesn't everyone?'

But Miranda wasn't letting him off that lightly.

'I don't know, Tony. I only know what I like, not what turns other people on. So how do you like it? Doggy-style, between her tits, or in her mouth? Or do you prefer boys . . . ?'

This, thought Alexa, was no ordinary management seminar. Where were the John Cleese videos and the dreary lectures on Maslow's Hierarchy of Needs? And this Ross woman wasn't your average course leader either. This wasn't going to be an easy ride.

'You see,' Miranda continued, 'we don't really know anything about each other, do we? And to really communicate we have to have a deeper knowledge of ourselves and others. That's what this seminar is all about. Creativity. And Communication.' She took a black marker and wrote the words in two-inch-high letters across the flip chart. 'So communicate with me.'

Miranda left Tony squirming and moved on, this time picking out the fat, balding guy in the corduroy trousers.

'You. Tell me about yourself.'

This one wasn't squirming, thought Alexa. He was getting off on the attention. It couldn't be every day that he met a sophisticated American beauty who wanted to know all about his dreary life.

'Clive Hanrahan. Financial director at Brutish Grand Opera. I'm thirty-nine, I'm a scratch golfer, my favourite food is Indonesian . . .'

'Married?'

'No.'

'Girlfriend?'

'Not . . . at the moment. But . . .' Clive was starting to look uncomfortable, thought Alexa, despite his initial bravado. It looked like Miranda had scored a direct hit.

'You're not gay, are you?'

Clive's face turned red as a blood-orange.

'Hell, no! Look, what *is* this?'

Perfectly unruffled, Miranda simply went on talking.

'So you say you're not gay, but you don't have a lover right now. Don't you like sex?'

'Of course I like sex! I'm a perfectly normal guy.'

'Oh good.' Miranda smiled benevolently as she settled herself on her chair and folded her hands in her lap. 'So tell me about your first sexual experience.'

A ripple of amusement mixed with surprise ran round the room. Raised eyebrows exchanged expressions that said, 'Thank God it's him and not me.' Alexa leaned forward to listen, caught somewhere between fascination and horror.

'Tell you *what*?' The high colour was beginning to drain away from Clive's pudgy face.

'About your first sexual experience,' repeated Miranda

18

sweetly. 'Tell me how you lost your virginity.'

'I don't have to do this.'

'True.'

He was halfway out of his seat, his hands on the arms.

'I can just get up and leave.'

'Any time you want.' Miranda's gaze was perfectly steady, her smile indulgent. 'But that would be such a pity. We're just beginning to get somewhere.'

Reluctantly, Clive sat down again.

'I still don't see what this has got to do with anything.'

'You will. Just relax. We're all friends here.'

Clive darted nervous glances around him. His eyes lingered longest on Alexa, as though her being there only added to his embarrassment. He coughed, and sat back in his chair.

'I was fifteen,' he began, his voice only half as loud as it had been when he'd first spoken.

'Go on,' said Miranda, running her long fingers through her hair and shaking it back from her forehead.

'There was this woman, Frida . . . she lived next door. She'd been a widow for years, she must've been about my mum's age, and she had a daughter, Megan she was called.'

'So did you seduce Megan, or was it the other way round?' asked the man to the right of Alexa.

Clive gave a cough which turned into a dry laugh.

'Neither,' said Miranda, her eyes very firmly fixed on Clive. 'It was her mother you had the hots for, isn't that right, Clive?'

His gaze snapped up to meet hers, half shocked, half furious, willing her to shut up.

'Yes,' he said at last.

'Go on then. Don't stop. Tell us what happened.'

Clive closed his eyes, shutting out the watching faces.

'She was a teacher, she used to help me with my homework sometimes. One night I went round to see her and she was alone in the house. She'd just got out of the bath, and all she was wearing was this white bathtowel, wrapped round her. It was so small it hardly covered her breasts, and it only reached to the tops of her thighs. When she sat down on the sofa, opposite me . . .'

'Tell me what you could see.'

'She was naked underneath. Her thighs were open and I could see everything. Everything! I mean, I'd seen pictures in girlie magazines and that kind of thing, but I'd never seen a real live woman's pussy. I was so hot I could hardly breathe, I had to loosen the top button of my shirt. She said, "Don't be shy, Clive, it's about time you learned how to please a woman." Then she got up and unwrapped the towel, and walked across the room towards me.

'She had the most fantastic body. Big breasts, really soft but firm, a tiny waist and round hips. And all this dark curly hair between her legs. I wanted to touch it and bury my face in it, and breathe in the scent of it, but I didn't dare. I just sat there not knowing what to do next.

'I remember I said, "What if somebody comes in?" She laughed, and said, "Megan won't be back for hours. Just relax, you'll make yourself ill if you let yourself get so tense." Then she unzipped my trousers and slid her hand inside.'

'And what happened then?' enquired Miranda.

'I . . . came in her hand.'

A ripple of muted laughter ran round the conservatory, but Miranda put up her hand.

'Go on. Tell me what happened next.'

Clive's breathing was coming in short, shallow gasps as he recalled that night, all those years ago.

'She started stroking my dick. I was a kid, it didn't take her long to get me excited again. I'd never felt anything like it, her fingers were so cool and strong. She seemed to know exactly what to do. It was miles better than wanking myself. And the next thing I know, I'm sitting there in her armchair and she's kneeling across my lap, with my dick inside her, bouncing up and down on top of me like a bloody spacehopper.'

'And how did it feel?'

'Like . . . heaven.'

There was a short silence. No one seemed to want to say anything, or look at anyone else. It was Miranda who broke the silence.

'Thank you, Clive. Very . . . stimulating.' The cool eyes scanned the audience. 'Now, who else has a story to tell?'

Alexa caught her breath. Not me, not me, choose anyone but me. Her heart pounded as Miranda looked her straight in the eye.

'How about you?'

Alexa recoiled, feeling all eyes turn on her.

'No. No, I don't think so.'

'Why not?'

'It's not really my thing.'

'Then maybe the exercise will do you good. Alexa, isn't it? Alexa de Maas?'

21

'How . . . ?'

'I like to do my homework. From what I hear you're a talented young woman, Alexa, but perhaps a little . . . repressed . . .'

'Repressed!' A lightning-bolt of anger shot through Alexa. A few minutes ago this had all been mildly amusing, but now things were getting uncomfortably personal.

'Of course, you don't *have* to participate, but I'm sure the directors of SuccessWorks would be pleased to hear that you'd got the fullest possible benefit from these training sessions.'

The smile remained completely steady. For a moment, Alexa thought about getting up and walking out. Then she thought of Damian: 'Look, listen, learn – then steal all her best ideas.' He wouldn't be pleased if she wimped out – and Piet would never let her hear the last of it.

OK, so this was a game she had to play. But there was nothing to say that she couldn't play it by her own rules.

'All right, what do you want to know?'

'Why don't you tell us all about the first time you made love?'

Alexa just about managed to suppress a smile. If that was what Miranda wanted to hear, she'd be sure to make it good. Bloody good.

'I was seventeen,' she said. 'And I'm not sure you can call it making love. I mean, we were in a TV studio at the time, with about two hundred other people.'

'Really?' There was a hint of genuine interest in Miranda's voice this time, and Alexa almost felt guilty.

'Uh-huh. I had this boyfriend – Andy – and somebody

gave him two tickets for a recording of *Top of the Pops*.
Actually, I was just about to chuck Andy, I was a bit sick
of him, but when I heard about the tickets I thought, stick
with him a bit longer, you never know who you might
meet.'

The kid in the next seat was round-eyed with interest.

'You got it on with him in a TV studio?'

Alexa laughed.

'Not me and him. Me and somebody else. I didn't even
know his name. We were in this crowd of kids dancing to
the Stone Roses, the lights were strobing and you couldn't
really tell what was going on or even who you were standing
next to.

'Andy was miles away, necking with some girl he'd met
on the train. I was dancing on my own. Then I felt these
hands . . . someone was behind me, pushing up my skirt.'

'Don't stop,' purred Miranda. 'You're doing so well.'

But Alexa had no intention of stopping. She was just
getting into her stride.

'I wriggled a bit, but then I thought, what the hell? It
felt nice. Whoever it was slid his hands inside my pants
and started rubbing and stroking my buttocks. I had no idea
it could feel so good, just having some bloke's hands on
your backside and his thumbs tickling the crease in
between.'

'What did he do next?' demanded Clive, back in the land
of the living now that the spotlight was off him.

'What do you think?' snapped back one of the younger
guys. 'He fucked her.'

'Actually,' Alexa corrected him, 'he pushed his finger

between my buttocks and slid it right inside my backside. I was afraid, I thought it'd hurt, but it felt wonderful.

'He was pressing right up against my back, I couldn't hear anything above the music but I could feel his breath on my cheek. He kissed the back of my neck and it made me shiver all over. I was so wet between my legs, and when he touched my pussy I thought I'd die, it felt so good.

'We moved together through the crowd, until I was right at the front, facing the stage. My belly was up against the wooden staging and my skirt was pulled right up at the back. I felt him push aside my panties, then this hard, warm thing slipped between my legs.

'I wasn't a complete innocent. I mean, I knew what it was and I knew what he was going to do with it, but can you imagine? There I was, sweet seventeen and never been fucked, about to give myself to some guy I'd never even seen!

'It was all I could do not to cry out when he took me. I bit my lip so hard it bled. But do you know what? Not one person noticed what we were up to. And to this day, I still have no idea who that guy was . . .'

She sat back in her chair, noting the looks of grudging admiration.

'And that's about it, end of story.'

Miranda pursed her immaculately-painted lips.

'Oh, I'm sure there's more, much more . . . but that's all we have time for this morning. I'll look forward to seeing you in tomorrow morning's session.'

Alexa gathered together her papers and switched off her tape recorder. That had been a waste of time. She wondered why Damian had been so keen on her attending the seminar – perhaps she'd underestimated his sense of humour. Or maybe . . . maybe there really was something in Miranda Ross's unorthodox management training techniques. And maybe if she stuck around, she'd find out what it was.

She lingered for a few minutes in the conservatory, gazing out at the gardens beyond. The morning frost had almost melted away, but there was still a faint sparkle on the close-cut lawn, like a sprinkle of diamond dust. Very festive. Her thoughts drifted back to Piet and their cosy house. She could be there right now, lying naked on a Chinese silk rug in front of the open fire, drinking Veuve Cliquot while Piet dressed her in a film of lingering kisses . . .

'Alexa de Maas?'

The voice came from a few feet behind her. She swung round, and came face to face with the dark-haired guy who had been watching her before the seminar began. The guy from the courtyard. Well over six feet tall, casually chic in a dark grey, boxy jacket and slim-cut black jeans, his body exuded lean athleticism; but it was his face which compelled attention, the angular features, blue-black hair and lightly-tanned skin giving him a faintly exotic appearance.

'Who wants to know?'

The eyes glinted under dark, arching brows. Now that she was standing so close, Alexa saw that they were a luminous sage-green, flecked with grey, compelling and not quite human.

'My name is Aidan Kane. You won't know me.'

'No?' I think I know all I want to know, she told herself.

25

I know that you like to fuck while complete strangers watch you.

'I was watching you back there.'

'I noticed.' Alexa finished packing up her stuff, and clicked shut her document case, picking it up, ready to leave. She couldn't resist a parting shot. 'Actually I was watching you too . . . yesterday afternoon.'

'You found it unsettling?'

Alexa gave a sarcastic laugh which concealed her discomfort. There was something she didn't like about Aidan Kane. Something dangerous that got right underneath her skin and threatened to insinuate itself into her soul like some exquisite cancer. Something she hated almost as much as she adored.

'Not particularly,' she lied.

'That was quite a performance you put on back there,' commented Kane.

'What's that supposed to mean?'

'Simply that I didn't believe a word you said. It was bullshit – but entertaining bullshit.'

Alexa shrugged. 'You can think what you like. Frankly I don't much care.'

'Do you want to know what I think? I think you have an impressively vivid sexual imagination. In fact, you strike me as quite an unusual woman.'

'So glad you find me entertaining,' snapped Alexa. 'Now, if you've nothing more important to say, I do have other seminars to go to.'

He stepped aside and she pushed past him, walking a little too quickly to the door in her haste to get away. As she reached the door, he called softly after her.

'Watch out for me, Alexa. I have a feeling our paths will cross again.'

Chapter 2

Alexa had all but made up her mind not to bother with Miranda Ross's second seminar. But some of the girls from a Birmingham agency were planning on going, and she was reckoning on safety in numbers. It was someone else's turn to be humiliated. Besides, she didn't much fancy the alternative: an afternoon of mud and bruises on the army-style assault course, 'building team-skills'.

Miranda Ross seemed pleased to welcome an extra five women to the seminar, though Clive and Tony were conspicuous by their absence. In fact, there was a rumour that Clive had had a blazing row with the conference director and gone back to London in a huff.

'Today, we're going to build on our knowledge of each other, breaking down the invisible barriers to better communication and inspired creativity. And I want to begin by looking at our fantasies . . .'

'What the hell has this got to do with "Creative Communication"?' demanded a male creative director, arms folded across his chest in aggressive non-cooperation.

'Nothing . . . and everything,' replied Miranda, turning over a page of the flip chart to reveal a diagram with four labelled boxes: 'Self', 'Others', 'Known' and 'Unknown'. 'Does anyone know what this is?'

'A Johari window?' suggested a tentative voice from the back.

'Good, yes. A Johari window. Let me explain. Our personalities are made up of four key types of information: what we know ourselves, what others know but we don't, what we and others both know, and what is completely unknown. The aim of every truly creative manager must be to increase the information which we and others know, and decrease the other three types. With me so far, Isidore?'

'S'pose,' grunted the creative director. 'But I still don't see—'

'In order to do this, you must "open" your Johari window as wide as you can. The more you can do this, the more confident and effective you will be as managers and co-workers.'

The elegant oriental girl sitting next to Alexa raised her hand.

'You want to raise a point, Suki?'

'These . . . windows. I can understand what you're saying about them, that we need to be more open in order to communicate. But what's this got to do with our fantasies?'

'Good point. But you see, Suki, fantasy is the very deepest, darkest, most secret part of our consciousness. It's the part we instinctively keep to ourselves. We don't want other people to know what we fantasise about. But if we can open up this part of ourselves, we can truly begin to communicate.'

'But there are some things . . . I mean, do we really have to tell *everything* about ourselves?'

'That's what I believe. In my opinion, all secrets are bad secrets.'

Uneasy noises and a shuffling of feet signalled a very English reaction to this bombshell. Miranda turned the page again. A single word shouted from the middle of the page, scrawled in red felt pen: 'FANTASY.'

'OK, pass round these sheets of paper. You have five minutes to write down your sexual fantasy. Then fold up the paper and put it into this box. When they're all in there we'll each draw one and read it out – so no one will know whose fantasy they're reading.'

This seemed to placate Isidore and his friends, and five minutes later there were fourteen folded sheets of paper in the box. Miranda passed it round and Alexa took one and unfolded it.

'OK Alexa, let's begin with you. What do you have?'

'"My fantasy is to be like a tiny baby again. I'm naked and suckling at a huge, milky breast. It's soft and warm and pink, and nothing exists but me and the breast. As I suckle I get more and more excited, my dick's getting stiff and throbbing, and at last it jerks and spurts, and I'm licking my own milky sperm from the breast."'

She crumpled it up and threw it back into the box, not sure whether to be amused, disgusted or both.

'Well that's a new one on me!' commented Suki.

'Pervert,' snorted Isidore. Which made Alexa even more certain that it was his fantasy she'd just read out.

The next to read was an advertising sales manager from Glasgow.

'"My fantasy is to be in bed with Keanu Reeves and Sean

Connery. Sean's dick is in my mouth and Keanu's giving me oral sex. When he's made me come twice we swap positions and I get up on my hands and knees, so Sean can take me from behind while I suck off Keanu . . .'"

This provoked a certain amount of embarrassment, until one of the Birmingham girls burst out laughing and gave the game away. Next came a couple of spanking fantasies and a rambling monologue about schoolgirls in navy-blue gym knickers. Pretty average stuff, thought Alexa. Ordinary people with dull fantasies, secrets hardly worth keeping. She listened to Isidore reading out her fantasy, and wondered how many of the others would guess it was hers.

"'Sometimes, I dream of being blindfolded and helpless. Unable to see my lover, unable to do anything but submit to his desires. I imagine lying there, luxuriating in the fear of what is going to happen to me, almost climaxing with anticipation . . .'"

And she supposed that that was depressingly ordinary, too. After all, didn't all women have domination fantasies, fantasy rape scenes they'd never dream of acting out in real life?

Gradually she lost interest, her attention drifting away. The sun was setting over the city and the sky was turning shades of deep pink and apricot, tinged with a dusky greyish blue. Soon it would be night, and the last vestiges of the sun's feeble warmth would have melted away. She imagined walking barefoot on the frozen grass, feeling it crunch and crackle underfoot; walking into the darkness towards some unseen lover who would do unspeakable things to her all-too-willing body.

And then she heard Aidan Kane's voice, and snapped instantly back to reality. She'd been avoiding him, had sat as far away as possible from him, had deliberately not looked at him. But the sound of his voice knifed into her consciousness, and there was something about what he was saying: not just the words themselves, but the way he was saying them.

And suddenly she knew. The fantasy he was reading out aloud wasn't anyone else's. It was his own.

'Fantasies,' he began softly, 'are of no value whatsoever unless you make them real. I believe in acting out all my fantasies.' The green-grey eyes met Alexa's gaze, and this time there was no escape. 'To me, the most erotic sensation in the world is the sensation of being in complete control. My lover is also my victim. I decide everything that is going to happen to her, I make the choice of giving her pleasure or pain.'

Somebody whistled softly, obviously impressed. Suki nudged Alexa's arm.

'Who do you think . . . ?'

Alexa didn't reply. She couldn't. She was lost in Kane's maze of words, the midnight-black fabric of his fantasy so skilfully woven that it might have been created especially for her. She felt as though he knew everything about her, could sense the unwilling excitement within her as he spoke of dominance and submission.

'In the darkness sight is no use at all,' Kane went on, his voice still quiet yet filled with an erotic charge which made Alexa's flesh tingle. 'You are blindfolded and helpless, you are forced to abdicate all responsibility to your lover. Your

33

master. You can survive by trusting your other senses, but those other senses can be deceived; and a master's pleasure may be in deceiving you.'

He paused, his breathing audible in the stunned silence of the conservatory. Outside, hail suddenly began to pour down out of the darkening sky, drumming a sinister tattoo on the glass roof.

'What's he going on about?' demanded one of the Birmingham girls in a loud stage-whisper. Alexa shook her head, waving her questions away.

'Darkness takes away reassurance and increases fear.' He smiled. 'And fear augments the body's capacity for pleasure – of that fact there can be no doubt at all . . .' Lowering the paper, he screwed it up in one hand and let it fall to the floor.

'Good God,' said somebody behind Kane, then fell silent. Even Miranda Ross looked taken aback.

'An unusual philosophy perhaps,' commented Kane, 'but interesting.' Alexa shivered as he turned towards her and looked her square in the face. 'Don't you think?'

Alexa skipped dinner and phoned home from the box in the lobby.

'Piet? I tried earlier, but you weren't in.'

'I was beginning to think you were having more fun without me.'

'Hardly. I haven't stopped working since I got here. If you can call it work.'

'So how's it going? Missing me yet?'

'You know I am.' Her thoughts drifted to crisp cotton sheets and soft pillows, to lying in bed and feeling Piet slide in beside her, his skin still hot and moist and fragrant from the shower. 'And in case you're wondering, no, I haven't developed a taste for fat, middle-aged advertising salesmen.'

'They can't *all* be unattractive.'

'No. I suppose they're not. But they're not you.'

'Yeah, but there has to be one . . . go on, tell me. Which one turns you on? Who are you going to see the New Year in with?'

Alexa laughed.

'Seminar notes and a jug of black coffee. I said I was coming here to work, and I meant it.' She wound the telephone flex round her fingers and leaned her cheek against the glass wall of the booth. 'How about you? Found something to keep you from getting bored?'

'As a matter of fact I have. She's twenty-three, blonde, and sexually insatiable.'

'You'd better be joking.'

Piet chuckled.

'Do you really think I'd tell you if I wasn't?'

As she put down the receiver, it occurred to Alexa that she didn't really know the answer to that. She had no idea what Piet got up to when she wasn't there. He was desirable, rich, spent half his life meeting glamorous people in glamorous places and had employed a string of blonde PAs who'd never heard of cellulite. It seemed highly unlikely that he'd stayed pure as the driven snow, yet he had the cheek to be possessive about her.

'Alexa!'

Suki Manderley was waving to her from the other side of the lobby. Alexa walked across, conscious that she looked rather ordinary in her plain black dress. By contrast, Suki was vibrantly sleek in scarlet Chinese silk embroidered with tiny yellow and blue flowers. Her glossy black hair was piled up in a loose chignon, secured with lacquered chopsticks.

'All dressed up and nowhere to go?' enquired Alexa, her eyes lingering on the wide, scooped neckline of Suki's dress, which seemed to mould itself so perfectly to her unusually full breasts.

'I had a dinner date with a business contact, but he cried off at the last minute. How about you? Fancy a drink in the bar?'

The bar was virtually deserted, save for a group of media analysts who were arguing the toss about high definition TV. Suki ordered two crème brûlées and a bottle of dessert wine, and she and Alexa went to sit at a corner table.

'I haven't seen you around much, except for the seminars,' commented Suki.

Alexa took a spoonful of her dessert, luxuriating in the contrast between soft, cold cream and hot, crunchy caramelised sugar.

'I've been writing up my notes in the evenings.' She wrinkled her nose. 'It's more interesting than sharing beer and dirty jokes with Clive and Isidore.'

She didn't add that she'd also been avoiding Aidan Kane, who seemed to be on the fringe of every discussion, a figure in the shadows of every sunny room. Even when she lay down on her bed and closed her eyes, he remained as an unseen presence, his words going round and round inside her head: 'I believe in acting out all my fantasies, turning them all into reality.'

Suki licked cream from her spoon. Alexa watched, idly fascinated by the wriggling pink tip of Suki's tongue, trickling with the rich, runny cream.

'It's bad enough having to bare your soul in public,' she said. 'I don't think I've ever been so embarrassed in all my life.'

'Miranda Ross's seminar, you mean?'

'Are all Americans so . . . upfront?'

'Only about ninety-eight per cent of them.' Alexa poured herself a second, really big glass of dessert wine. 'Mmm, Orange Muscat and Flora, how decadent.'

'We deserve it. We've been working hard.'

Alexa found herself tracing the line of Suki's neck and shoulder, the broad neckline baring an expanse of smooth, slightly olive skin. The wall-lamps picked out tiny hairs, soft and faint as the down on peach-skin, and Alexa had a sudden, irrational desire to run her tongue down the side of Suki's cheek, over her jawline and into the crook of her throat, feeling the breath vibrate through her as she spoke. There was no doubt about it, Suki Manderley was a very attractive, very desirable woman. If, of course, you happened to be into that sort of thing.

'By the way, Suki. It's a few hours early, but Happy New Year.'

Suki smiled and nodded. 'Happy New Year.'

Alexa drained her glass. She knew you were supposed to sip dessert wine, but it was too delicious to linger over. And it was deceptively strong, its thick, honeyed elixir making it all too easy to forget how much you'd drunk. The second bottle was soon uncorked, the conversation loosening up as the evening went on. The crème brûlée lay half-eaten and entirely forgotten.

'Those fantasies . . .' murmured Suki. 'Did you listen to them?'

'Of course.'

'And did they shock you?'

Alexa fiddled with the stem of her glass. She was secretly imagining it as the stalk of Suki's nipple, grown hard and erect between her fingers. Or her own clitoris, drawn into a swollen spike between Suki's peony-red lips.

'Actually, I thought most of them were very . . . ordinary. Didn't you?'

'Ordinary! All that stuff about wanting to be a baby . . . ?'

'Yeah, but most of them just want to spank schoolgirls' bottoms, or have Sharon Stone give them a blow-job. Guys like that don't have any imagination, they get all their fantasies out of girlie mags and cheap videos.'

Suki shifted a little closer to Alexa. Their legs touched.

'And what about your fantasy, Alexa? Which one was it?'

Alexa pressed her thigh against Suki's, answering the first, clumsy caress. Their heat met and mingled.

'Can't you guess?'

Suki contemplated the last of the wine, sitting in the bottom of the bottle; then picked it up and emptied it into the two glasses. Alexa watched her drink, entranced by the way her throat contracted as she swallowed, the way her breasts undulated beneath her dress at the slightest movement of her arm. There was something very snake-like about the smooth slyness of Suki's body, and the darting movements of her tongue as she lapped the last drops of wine from the rim of the glass.

'I . . . have a fantasy,' said Suki slowly.

'Everybody does.' And right now, thought Alexa, my fantasy is sitting beside me, sleekly sensual in gift-wrapped silk.

'No, not the one I wrote for the seminar, another one.' Suki's thigh slid smoothly over Alexa's. 'A fantasy I'd never confess . . .'

Suki's almond eyes gave nothing away, but her nipples were hard and prominent beneath the embroidered silk of her dress. Alexa laid a hand upon hers and smiled.

'We *all* have that fantasy,' she said softly. And she felt Suki's hand slip lightly from between her fingers as the dark-eyed girl got to her feet in a swish of scarlet silk.

'Shall we go to your room? You can tell me all about it.'

Suki clicked on the light and closed the door behind her.

'I've been waiting for this . . . oh Alexa, you just can't know how much I've wanted you . . .'

Taking Alexa's hands, she drew her into a kiss. Alexa responded, at first hesitantly, unused to the feel of another woman's breasts against hers, the rounded swell of another woman's backside under her hand. Suki took Alexa's face in her hands and drew back.

'You've never done this before?'

'I never thought – well, I never thought I'd want to. But I wondered sometimes what it would be like . . .'

She closed her eyes briefly as Suki kissed her again, this time reaching behind her and drawing down the zipper on her little black dress. Its own weight carried it downwards, skimming her body lightly as it slid down to form a cloud of black chiffon around her feet.

'This is what it's like,' whispered Suki, kissing her bare shoulders and easing open the catch on her black lace bra. 'It's better than paradise.'

Alexa's head swam. She had an extremely pleasant sensation of slight unreality, just drunk enough to leave behind every lingering inhibition and think of nothing but the pursuit of physical gratification. She let out a delicious giggle as her bra peeled away and Suki's cool hands cupped her breasts, trapping her nipples between finger and thumb and subjecting them to the most unforgiving pleasure.

'Suki, oh Suki, this is too much . . .'

'But we've only just started. I'm going to show you something tonight, Alexa. I'm going to show you that you don't need a man to have a good time.'

This time it was Alexa who initiated the kiss, sliding her hands round Suki's backside and easing up her dress as their lips met, tongues jousting for supremacy. The tastes of sweet wine and double cream mingled with the muskiness of animal scents, potent and intoxicating.

Alexa's fingers slid up Suki's thighs and met the small, round globes of her buttocks, completely and defiantly bare to the touch. She heard Suki murmur her pleasure and felt her slide her feet a little way apart; and, intrigued and excited by this voyage of discovery, Alexa let her fingers stray into the deep, moist seam between Suki's arse-cheeks.

The thin string of her thong made a parody of modesty. It was the easiest thing in the world to push it aside and run a fingertip lightly down the warm furrow, feeling the tiny eye of Suki's anus wink and quiver at the touch. A few inches lower, and she met the honeypot of her sex, wet and sticky with the juices of her longing.

'Push your finger inside. Right inside,' murmured Suki. 'I want you to feel how much I want you.'

It felt strange to slide a finger deep into another woman's pussy, thought Alexa, to feel her muscles contract and suck you in. But it was a delicious captivity, and the hardness of Suki's body was rubbing against Alexa's pubis, exciting her in ways she had hardly believed possible. She was sober enough to know that she shouldn't be doing this, drunk enough not to give a damn, and lucid enough to understand that pleasure was a thousand times more satisfying when it was mingled with a little wickedness.

Suki let out a soft moan: 'Darling bitch.'

Her fingernails raked down Alexa's back, gouging and striating the skin, making it tingle and sting. Alexa writhed in excitement, grinding belly against belly, feeling the sensations multiply in her swollen sex. It would be so easy to bring herself to orgasm, simply by rubbing body against body.

But Suki had other ideas. Her fingers hooked under Alexa's black panties and jerked them down.

'You don't need these. All you need is your beautiful, naked body.'

'Then I want you naked too.'

'Undress me. Go on, I'm waiting.'

It was like undressing a beautiful doll; peeling away the dress from the long, waxy-smooth limbs to reveal the white g-string, hold-up stockings and nothing else. Suki's magnificent breasts were unfettered, their brown-tipped crests pert and hard.

'You're beautiful,' whispered Alexa, smoothing her hands down over Suki's flanks and bending her face to take one leathery nipple into her mouth.

She had never tasted a woman's nipple in her life before; had no idea that it would excite her so much to feel the ridged, toughened flesh on her tongue and taste its light seasoning of sweat. But with each flick of her tongue across the tip, her clitoris throbbed and swelled, pulsing to a synchronistic rhythm. And Suki unfastened Alexa's hair and let it tumble down over her shoulders, stroking it like the mane of a favourite mare.

'Oh yes, Alexa, oh yes, I knew all along this was what you wanted too.'

Alexa allowed Suki's nipple to escape from her mouth. Her lips were wet with the delicious taste of her.

'There's something else I want,' she said, lightly caressing Suki's breasts. 'Something that will make this more exciting for me.'

'Anything.'

'You're sure?'

'I told you. Anything.'

Walking across to the dressing table, Alexa slid open one of the drawers and reached inside.

She took out a black velvet evening scarf, perfectly plain except for silk tasselling at the ends. It felt good in her hands, soft and luxurious and perhaps just a little menacing. She held it out to Suki.

'Take it.'

Suki took it with a questioning look.

'You want me to wear this?'

Alexa shook her head. Oh no, that wasn't it at all.

'No. Not you. Me.' She kissed Suki lightly, pleadingly, on the brow. 'I want you to blindfold me with it.'

Chapter 3

There were two women on the bed: one clearly oriental, the other tall with red-brown hair, pale skin and a blindfold over her eyes. Both were naked, and seemed oblivious to anything beyond their own immediate gratification.

'Well, well, well,' said Aidan Kane, freeze-framing the VCR and throwing the last of the photographs onto Alexa's bedside table. 'Seen enough?'

Alexa stared at the frozen image on the screen for long, agonising seconds. There was no doubt about it, the two figures on the bed were herself and Suki Manderley; the thick velvet blindfold did nothing to disguise Alexa's identity, even if you discounted the tiny devil tattoo on her right buttock.

'Well?' enquired Kane coolly.

Horrified paralysis turned to fury, and she rounded on him with a face full of hatred.

'Where the hell did you get those pictures?'

'They were taken using a camera concealed in the light fitting. Rather cleverly done, don't you think?'

'Clever! You've been spying on me, and all you can do is boast about it? What kind of a bloody pervert are you?'

Kane laughed, his grey-flecked green eyes flicking back

45

towards the two women on the TV screen. Alexa was pictured on her hands and knees, thighs wide apart while Suki lapped, kitten-like, at her pussy.

'The same kind as you, from what I can see.'

'You bastard.' Alexa made a grab for the phone. 'I'm going to call the police.'

Kane shook his head.

'I very much doubt it. I mean, would you and Mr de Maas really want this whole sordid business to come out in the press? He's an influential man in the financial world. The tabloids would have a field day.' Ejecting the video cassette from the VCR, he slipped it into his inside pocket. 'You can keep the photos, I have the negatives, of course.'

'I knew you were bad news, the minute I set eyes on you.'

'Really? I had the distinct impression you were sexually attracted to me.'

He didn't smile, but she knew he was mocking her. Alexa's brain worked quickly.

'What is it you want? Money? Because I think you should know it's my husband who's rich, not me.'

'So I've heard. But no, it's not money I want.'

'What then?'

Kane glanced towards the television screen, then back at Alexa.

'You.'

Taken aback, she just stared at him for several moments.

'What did you say?'

'You heard me the first time. If I were you, I'd stop behaving like a petulant child, shut up and listen to me. You don't want your husband to know about what you've been up to, do you?'

Alexa glared back at him from the other side of the bed, refusing to give him the satisfaction of a reply. Kane obligingly supplied it himself.

'No, of course you don't. He's a rather possessive man, is Mr Piet de Maas, or so I've heard. As I see it, he wouldn't be too pleased to hear about your sexual exploits. Would he?'

'Why don't you tell me?' demanded Alexa with venom. 'Since you seem to have it all worked out.'

'Very well, if that's the way you want to play it. I'm going to put a proposition to you, A sexual solution. A perfectly civilised arrangement, which needn't cause you any more than a slight . . . inconvenience.' He smiled. 'I have a suspicion you might even enjoy it.'

The eyes travelled Alexa's body from her feet upwards. She wished she could control the slight shaking of her limbs, heartily detested her own weakness in still, in spite of everything, finding Aidan Kane compellingly attractive in a repulsive kind of way. If Piet de Maas was a golden-haired Adonis, then Aidan Kane was Satan himself. But there might be a certain perverse excitement in being desired by the Devil . . .

'Well?'

'In return for my silence, you will give yourself to me, to do with as I please, on one day in every month.'

Alexa's lip curled in a sneer.

'Give myself to you? You're crazy.'

'What I am, Alexa, is single-minded. It's not often I find

a woman who stimulates my creative imagination as much as you do. You ought to be flattered.'

Kane thrust his hand into the pocket of his mandarin-collared jacket and took out a card. He laid it on the bed, in front of Alexa. It bore no name, no address, no useful information whatsoever, just a gold portcullis on a red background.

'What the hell is this supposed to be?' demanded Alexa, flicking it over and finding it blank.

'The next time you receive one of these cards, it will be time. Until then, you will wait, be patient. You will not attempt to contact me, and if you try you will fail.'

'Get out of my room,' snapped Alexa. Kane stood his ground, a flicker of amusement playing about his large, sensual mouth.

'What a little wildcat you think you are,' he murmured.

'Get out and go to hell!'

Alexa swung a punch at Kane, half-intending to scratch out those maddening eyes; but he caught her fist in mid-flight and – to her complete rage and humiliation – pressed her fingers to his lips in a parody of a kiss.

'We will meet again. Soon,' he said, and opening the door he stepped out into the corridor. His dark hair took on an unearthly, bluish sheen under the night-lights, chiaroscuro turning his eyes into no more than dark shadows.

'Not if I see you first,' spat back Alexa, more from bravado than conviction.

But Aidan Kane simply blew her an ironic kiss, turned and sauntered towards the staircase, looking like he didn't have a care in the world.

* * *

The rest of the conference went by with agonising slowness. Only two days to go, but they might as well have been two weeks. Once or twice Alexa even considered throwing all her clothes into her suitcase and taking the next train home. Only there wasn't a next train: the whole world was on holiday and she was stuck at Boroughbridge Hall till the bitter end.

There was only one good thing about those two days: having got what he wanted, Aidan Kane seemed to have disappeared into thin air. At least Alexa didn't have to put up with him watching her, following her, winding her up until she almost believed she wanted him in her bed.

But he was harder to get out of her mind. Even as she filed into the conservatory for Miranda Ross's final seminar, she was instinctively glancing back over her shoulder, expecting him to emerge from behind one of the pillars, arms folded and smiling.

Miranda Ross strode into the seminar and took charge with a snap of her fiercely-manicured fingers. Turning the page of the flip chart, she revealed a single word:

'WHY?'

'This is our last session together,' she began, drawing a series of circles around the word in red pen. 'I've asked you to reveal your fantasies, your hopes, your fears, your most secret inner truths. And I suppose you're wondering if I'm simply some kind of voyeuristic pervert, or if there is in fact a point to it all.'

The rosy mouth curled up at the corners.

'So what do *you* think?'

Alexa jolted into alertness as she realised that Miranda was pointing straight at her.

'Well . . .' she stuttered, thinking on her feet. 'I suppose it's all designed to make us better communicators . . . by making us more open . . .'

'You don't sound convinced,' commented Miranda, scrawling 'communication' and 'openness' underneath 'WHY?'

'So convince me.'

Miranda stepped down from the platform and walked slowly back and forth in front of the line of chairs – now whittled down from twelve to a core of six die-hard masochists.

'The point of this seminar programme has been to expose all the barriers which exist between yourselves, each other and the people you will encounter in your working lives. By exposing these barriers, we show the whole you instead of just the you that you'd like to project.'

'And what's the point of that?' demanded Isidore, more than a hint of suspicion in his voice.

'When people see the whole you, provided they can accept what they see, they *trust* you.' Miranda wrote 'trust' on the flipchart and underlined it three times. 'Complete, one-hundred-per-cent trust. It's worth its weight in gold. It builds teams, it allows people to get on with their jobs without wasting valuable time and energy wondering what other people are getting up to when their backs are turned.'

'So trust promotes greater efficiency? That's what you're saying?'

'Precisely, Suki. When you trust your co-workers, you

stop worrying about their competence and their loyalty. And that allows you to delegate tasks you're responsible for, but don't have time to do yourself. And of course, as a last resort . . .'

Miranda picked up her handbag and clicked open the catch. Reaching inside, she drew something out. Something hard, black, shiny and menacing.

'Bloody hell,' hissed Isidore. Alexa tensed. Suki stared open-mouthed at the pistol, its long glossy muzzle lovingly cradled in the palm of Miranda's hand. As they watched, breath caught in their throats, Miranda raised the pistol, took careful aim at Isidore's head and pulled the trigger.

With a soft popping sound, a little white flag shot out of the gun-barrel. On it, in black capitals, were written two words: 'YOU'RE FIRED.'

'. . . as a last resort,' repeated Miranda with a superior smile, 'trust allows you to use and abuse other people, simply because they trust you not to.'

Alexa's last night at Boroughbridge Hall would have been a non-event, if not for Miranda Ross's toy gun, and the diverting company of Suki Manderley.

Alexa was nothing if not practical. Her guilty secret was out, Aidan Kane had the photos to prove it, and there was nothing to be gained from sitting alone in her room. Besides, what better way could there be to find out if Suki was in league with Kane, than to accept an invitation to her room and break down her resistance with pure pleasure? As an afterthought, she took the velvet blindfold and slipped it into her handbag before locking the door of her room behind her.

Suki was waiting for her in white satin camiknickers, with champagne and a bath full of hot bubbles. They kissed, passing a mouthful of chilled Moët between their eager mouths.

'You came,' said Suki, coming up for air. Alexa stroked the single, dark plait which fell forward over Suki's shoulder, swishing across her breasts like a mare's tail.

'You thought I wouldn't?'

'I thought maybe I'd frightened you off.'

Alexa laughed.

'Remember what Miranda Ross said about trust? Complete trust? I trusted you with my pleasure.'

'I'm flattered.' Suki took Alexa's hand and led her towards the bath. 'First I'm going to bathe you, then I'm going to give you an aromatherapy massage. It's our last night, I want you to remember it.'

'As if I could forget.' Alexa allowed Suki to unbutton her shirt and trousers, and peel them from her body. Reaching behind her, she unhooked the catch of her bra and slid the straps down over her arms.

'Suki . . . do you trust me?'

'Of course.'

'Enough to let me do whatever I like to you?' Alexa caught Suki's wrist and, rotating it so her hand was face-up, ran her tongue over her palm from fingertips to wrist. 'Enough to let me blindfold you?'

Still holding Suki by the waist, Alexa pulled her towards her and lavished kisses on her upturned face, her throat, the deep valley between her breasts.

'Anything . . .' whispered Suki, eyes closed.

Alexa felt a surge of arousal, deep in her belly, as she allowed her lips and tongue to explore Suki's smooth skin. It was supple and fragrant, almost as delicate as a child's, with a moist freshness which enchanted and seduced.

'You gave me such pleasure the other evening,' murmured Alexa into the crook of Suki's neck. 'Now I'm going to repay the compliment.'

The blindfold lay, neatly folded, in her Dior bag. Such an innocent thing, nothing more sinister than a strip of black cotton velvet, tasselled with silk. But already it had proved its worth as an instrument of sensual fantasy.

She pressed the velvet scarf against Suki's eyes and tied it behind her head.

'Can you see?'

'Not a thing.'

'Promise?'

'I swear. I'm yours now, Alexa, you can do whatever you like to me.'

'. . . give yourself to me, to do whatever I like . . .'

The echo of Aidan Kane's words sent a frisson of half-remembered fear through Alexa's body. Had he meant what he said? Would he carry out his threat, or was it all some elaborate joke, maybe even part of Miranda Ross's outrageous management training programme? But Aidan Kane hadn't seemed like the sort of man who'd care for practical jokes. Cursing him, she set about exacting a kind of sensual revenge on Suki Manderley's defenceless body.

'Get into the bath, Suki.'

'I can't see . . .'

'I'll guide you. You'll just have to trust me.'

Stepping naked into the hot, scented water, Alexa took Suki's hands and guided her into the bath.

'I . . . I'm going to fall!'

'Don't be afraid, I won't let you fall.'

Alexa's lips trailed kisses down Suki's bare arms as she pulled her down until she was kneeling in the bath. By now the white silk camisole was soaked through and perfectly transparent, clinging to her breasts like a coating of frosted sugar, but beneath the surface of the water floating and fanning out like the petals of a waterlily, offering glimpses of Suki's slender thighs and tangle of close-cropped curls.

Pressing her lips against the wet silk, Alexa took Suki's nipple into her mouth. It was hard and mobile beneath the smooth fabric, her whole breast quivering and dancing to the rhythm of Alexa's kisses. As Suki's breathing quickened, Alexa let her tongue flick mischievously across the erect crest.

'Oh. Oh Alexa, what are you doing? That feels . . . it feels so strange!'

Alexa smiled to herself. She knew how it felt to be helpless in the darkness, to have no idea what was happening, or what curious sensations might follow, piling layer upon layer of stolen, abandoned pleasure. And she let her right hand slide down Suki's belly, creeping closer and closer to the heartland of her sex.

Suki shivered and squirmed as Alexa pushed her back, lower and lower into the water.

'No, stop! Stop, I'll drown!'

'Trust me.'

'The water – it's getting so high, I'm afraid!'

'Just trust me.'

The trailing tassels of the blindfold were floating on the surface of the water, Alexa supporting Suki's head as she knelt between her thighs, pushed aside the loose gusset of the camiknickers and slid her fingers up to the apex of her sex. Even in the surrounding water it was easy to distinguish it from the thicker, slippery texture of the juice which trickled and oozed over the coral-pink flesh. And now Suki lay helpless in her arms, the victim of her own desperate lust, as Alexa drew mischievous circles on her inner pussy-lips, almost but never quite touching the tiny jutting tongue of her clitoris.

'Please,' whimpered Suki.

'Tell me what you want.'

'Please . . .' That was all she could say. The power of speech had soaked away from her, drained out into the surrounding water. The scent of damask roses filled Alexa's head, making her dizzy and intensifying her excitement, making it all feel more unreal than ever.

'It's all right, I *know* what you want.'

And drawing a deep breath into her lungs, Alexa plunged her face under the surface of the water, pressing her lips savagely about the stalk of Suki's clitoris. As Alexa let go of her head, Suki climaxed with a sudden, desperate cry, her arms thrashing wildly as she fought to stay afloat, water flooding her mouth and soaking the blindfold, dragging her down at the summit of pleasure.

Alexa scooped her up in her arms, pressing her wet mouth against Suki's.

'All you have to do is trust me,' she whispered. And kneeling astride Suki's bare thigh, she pressed the slick wetness of her sex against the hard flesh, and rode herself to orgasm.

On the train journey from York to Cheltenham, Alexa felt fantasy gradually ebbing away as cold reality forced its way back into her consciousness.

Piet would be waiting for her at the station, ready to drive her back to their home in Cirencester. He'd be sure to ask her how she'd got on, how she'd enjoyed the conference. And what was she going to tell him – something or nothing or everything?

Not everything, that was for sure. Aidan Kane had been right about Piet. He was possessive, proud, used to being in sole ownership of whatever he chose to possess. She'd be mad to tell him about the two nights of decadence she'd spent with Suki Manderley, who was clearly just as much an innocent victim as she was, or about Kane and his outlandish proposition. But if she didn't . . . Kane would. Unless, of course, he'd been bluffing all along.

Panic turned to a lead weight in her stomach as the train slid alongside platform two. There was no going back, not that she'd want to in any case. She'd had enough of Boroughbridge Hall and Miranda Ross's seminars to last a lifetime.

'Piet!'

Alexa ran up to the silver-grey Mercedes and he wound down the window. She bent down to kiss him and he held her head between his strong hands, taking complete control of the kiss. It was Piet who decided when it would end.

'What kept you? You're fifteen minutes late!'

She slid into the passenger seat and threw her suitcase into the back.

'A speck of dust on the line or something. Is that all you can say? Haven't you missed me?'

He grinned and tossed back his slightly wavy blond hair. He looked, thought Alexa, just like a golden lion with that corn-blond hair and those burnished-gold eyes. His hand slid up her thigh and pushed back her skirt.

'Just you wait till I get those knickers off you, I'll teach you to go off and abandon me on New Year's Eve! Now, hold on tight – I've got to drop you off home and then drive to Malmesbury.'

'What!'

Piet shrugged, easing the Merc out into the one-way system and heading out towards the M4.

'It's Gregor. You remember him, don't you?'

'Gregor who?'

'Gregor Potemkin. From the Pan-Slavonic Bank of St Petersburg. He's staying over in Malmesbury on business, and it's Russian Orthodox Christmas today – I said I'd drive him to church.'

Alexa shook her head.

'Must be the first time you've been to church since . . .'

'Since never. My parents were Humanists, remember?'

'Might have guessed you'd be a heathen. You merchant bankers are all the same. No more morals than . . . than . . .'

Piet darted her a sidelong glance.

'Than a graphic designer in a PR agency?'

Touché, thought Alexa. Could Piet read her mind? Could he tell that she had something to hide? They drove on for several miles in relative silence. The frost had melted and the countryside looked wet and dingy. Suddenly a mad impulse overtook Alexa.

'Stop the car.'

'What!'

'Stop the car, I know you're in a hurry but this is important.'

'All right, all right.' Piet signalled left and steered the car into a lay-by, switching off the engine. 'Now, what's this all about?'

Alexa's mouth was dry, her heart pounding. This was crazy, why hadn't she just kept her mouth shut?

'I've got something to tell you.'

'Go on then.'

'You know you accused me of spending New Year's Eve with another man?'

'That was just a joke.'

'Yeah, well, I didn't.'

'Didn't what?'

'It wasn't a man. It was another woman.'

She held her breath, waiting for the storm to break. She knew Piet had a temper, he might do anything – but surely anything was better than living in the shadow of Aidan Kane . . .

'What was she called?' demanded Piet softly.

'Suki. Does it matter?'

To Alexa's surprise, Piet's expressionless face softened into a smile.

'Of course it matters. I want you to tell me all about it. All about her. All about what you did.'

'You . . .'

Piet's hand returned to Alexa's thigh, this time sliding higher and higher until it reached and rested on the plump hummock of her pubis, thinly veiled by rose-coloured satin.

'Everything.' His breathing was audible, slightly hoarse. With a shiver of sudden realisation, Alexa understood why. He wasn't angry. He was turned on. All that late-night talk about making up a threesome with another woman, perhaps it had been more than just a bedtime game after all. 'I want you to tell me everything. And then I'm going to take you into that field over there, push you up against that tree and fuck you till you beg for mercy.'

Alexa lay across the rumpled sheets on the king-size bed, basking in the afterglow of excellent, exhilarating sex. Piet's unexpected reaction to her confession about Suki had left her stunned, intrigued, delighted. With each new detail she'd told him he'd become more and more aroused, more and more inspired in his lovemaking. They'd never done it in a field before, barely fifty yards from a main road in the perishing January cold. It had been good; no, better than good. Maybe they ought to go right back there and do it again.

Once back home, they'd started all over again, Piet demanding to be told the story once more, even acting out the part where Alexa had made Suki kneel before her on the bathroom carpet and lick out her pussy. His enthusiasm had left Alexa glowing all over, wickedly happy and tingling with physical gratification.

And of course there was another thing to be thankful for.

She was free, free of Aidan Kane and his ridiculous 'proposition'. Now that Piet knew everything there was to know about what she'd done with Suki Manderley, she had nothing to fear from Aidan's threats. You couldn't blackmail someone when the cat was already out of the bag.

Piet called up to her, on the mezzanine, from the kitchen below.

'Coffee or champagne?'

She rolled onto her belly and propped herself up on her elbows.

'Oh champagne, definitely. I'm feeling decadent. Shall I run us a bath?'

'Sounds great. I'll be up in a minute, I've just got a couple of phone calls to make.'

Alexa stretched like a she-cat and bounced off the bed. Going into the bathroom, she turned on the hot tap and splashed in a generous amount of foaming bath oil. Then she went back into the bedroom in search of clean underwear, humming to herself as she slid open the drawer.

And then her heart stopped in mid-beat. For there, lying underneath her absolute favourite pair of Janet Reger knickers, was an envelope. A small, red envelope, decorated with the outline of a gold portcullis.

Chapter 4

Alexa stared down at the red envelope in her hands, feeling its smug smoothness between her fingers. She hadn't even opened it yet. Somehow opening it would make it all too real – and what was it Aidan Kane had said, about turning all his fantasies into reality? Well, she wasn't going to be the next in a long line of wet dreams, whatever he might think.

In the next room, she heard Piet on the phone, his voice terse and irritable.

'What do you mean, you don't know anything about him? If you don't know anything about Aidan Kane, then find it out.'

He crashed the receiver back onto the hook and came back into the room.

'Well?'

'Nothing.'

Alexa kissed him on the cheek and drew him down onto the rumpled coverlet.

'Never mind. It doesn't really matter, does it?'

'Doesn't matter?' Piet's face registered incomprehension. 'Of course it bloody well matters!'

'No, no it doesn't, really it doesn't.' Alexa stroked the curls on the back of his neck, soothing him, making him purr like the angry lion he was. 'We can just ignore it, tear it up, forget about it. I mean, you know everything, so Aidan Kane has nothing to blackmail me with any more, does he?'

Piet sighed and patted her hand, as though she were a slightly retarded child.

'Of course we can't forget it. This Kane has got too close to me for that.'

'Too close to *you!*'

'Yes, Alexa. Me.' Piet slid his arm round Alexa's waist and, very slowly and very tenderly, lowered her onto the bed, covering her with his powerful body. 'I can't allow that, you must understand.'

'I don't understand anything,' murmured Alexa, gazing up into Piet's face as he bent low over her and ran his tongue lightly between her breasts.

'The thing is, Alexa, you'll have to . . .' He paused, as though trying to find the best way of saying something unpalatable. 'You'll have to string him along, just for a little while.'

Alexa froze, not wanting to guess what Piet might mean by 'stringing Kane along'.

'Now hold on, Piet . . .'

'Just for a little while, I promise, until my contacts have had a chance to find out what sort of game he's playing.'

'You're telling me you want me to do what he says? Go with him and be his . . . his *plaything*?' Outraged, she wriggled out of Piet's grasp and rolled to the other side of the bed.

Piet's voice was soft and coaxing as he stroked her shoulder, easing down the flimsy robe of Venice lace he'd brought her back from some business trip or other.

'If the tables were turned, I'd do it for you . . .'

Alexa turned furious eyes on Piet.

'Oh yes, I bet you would. In fact I wouldn't be surprised if you already do. Do you think I haven't noticed how all your PAs have long legs, big tits and no brain?' She regretted the outburst straight away. For a start, she was the one in the wrong, not Piet. And he looked so . . . so wounded, like he'd asked her some tiny favour and she'd told him to go screw himself. 'Oh Piet . . .'

His lips traced the path of his fingers, easing down the robe and replacing it with a filmy covering of kisses and tiny, delicate bites.

'For me?'

'Piet, I can't . . . you don't know what you're asking. He's . . . I'm afraid of him, Piet!'

'No harm will come to you, I'll make sure of that.' The wiry hairs on his chest brushed against her bare back as he slipped his hands under her belly and cupped her sex in his palm. 'I promise.'

Alexa felt all the strength and defiance ebbing out of her.

'I hate you,' she moaned, wriggling like an eel on the hook of Piet's index finger, which had somehow found its wicked way into the moist haven between her thighs. 'I hate you . . . so much . . .'

But it was a complete fabrication, and Piet knew it. He had her where he wanted her, and it was where she wanted to be, too. Rolling her onto her back, Piet reached out for the envelope and put it into her hands.

'Go on. Open it.'

'I'm not going to. You *know* I'm not going to do this!'

'What harm is there in opening the envelope? Aren't you curious to know what's inside? Maybe it's empty.'

It wasn't empty, of course. Even before she'd torn it open, Alexa could feel the outline of a rectangle of thin card. She slid it out and read the black, looping letters.

'Well?'

'Gloucester Docks,' she read in a halting voice. 'The Antiques Centre, Sunday afternoon.'

She took some convincing. Or at least, on the face of it she put up a fight. To do anything less would have seemed downright indecent. She told Piet she hated him, despised him, that he was nothing better than a pimp. But the words just bounced off him, and they both knew she didn't mean them. Because Alexa was driven by more than petty resentment; she had a burning desire to get her own back on Aidan Kane.

At lunchtime on Sunday, she put on her ankle-length cashmere coat over a smart olive-green skirt, and took the car-keys from the hall table.

'I could come with you,' suggested Piet.

Alexa shook her head.

'If I'm doing this at all, I'm doing it on my own.'

'Then take this.' Piet reached into his pocket and took out a small square of black plastic, with a red button in the middle. 'It's a personal alarm. If things get bad, if he frightens you, if he does anything at all – just press it, someone will be there in a few minutes. I've . . . made arrangements.'

Alexa glanced at it and dropped it into her pocket. Underneath she was quaking, but she wasn't going to show Piet that she was afraid.

'I'll see you later, then.'

She was going to walk straight out of the house, but Piet caught her arm and pulled her back, swinging her round to face him and holding her to him.

'You look incredible. Do you know that? I don't think I've ever wanted you more than I want you right now.'

There was an intensity in his eyes that made Alexa shiver; a vibrancy, an excitement. This was turning him on, she thought to herself. He'd always had a fantasy about inviting another woman into their bed, just one of those innocent mind-games men liked to play to spice up their love-lives – or so she'd thought until now.

Well, now he was about to share her with another man, and to her shame, Alexa found that even in her anger and fearful expectation, the idea was more exciting than terrifying, much more appealing than it had any right to be.

They kissed lingeringly, then Alexa pulled away, slipping her gloved hand from between Piet's fingers. She stepped outside and closed the door silently behind her.

Everything was white, even the sky. Snow was tumbling down like goose-feathers out of a burst pillow, last night's snowfall crunching under the heels of her boots as she walked to her jeep and opened the driver's door. Only an idiot would drive to Gloucester on a day like this. Then again, only an idiot would go along with this insane rendezvous.

Perhaps he wouldn't turn up. She drove slowly onto the

main road, tyres struggling to bite on the greying slush. Perhaps he just wanted to send her on a wild-goose chase, teach her a lesson for not falling into bed with him at the first opportunity.

She knew Gloucester quite well. SuccessWorks had done the PR for one of the museums in the restored docklands development, and Alexa had designed some of the publicity brochures. She wondered why Aidan Kane had chosen this, of all places; and reassured herself that he could hardly do anything very terrible in public.

Parking close to the maritime museum, she drew her coat round her and walked towards the antiques centre, one of the converted warehouses strung along the waterfront. The wind was whipping up the snowflakes now, seizing the breath from Alexa's lungs and flinging it back in her face in a stinging handful of ice.

There were few people about, just one or two groups of frozen tourists, scurrying between the Opie Collection and the indoor café, studiously avoiding the tall ships bobbing dangerously in the dock. As she got closer and closer to the antiques centre, Alexa felt a knot of panic twisting in the pit of her stomach. I can't go through with this, she thought, her fingers briefly touching the alarm in her pocket for reassurance. I can't, I can't!

But her feet kept on carrying her slowly towards the five-storey warehouse with the garish yellow sign, towards the double doors and the invisible eyes she was convinced must be watching her from all sides, laughing themselves senseless at her stupidity.

Kane wasn't outside, waiting for her. Perhaps he'd meant

inside the centre. But the doors were shut.

'Excuse me?'

The girl in the yellow anorak turned round.

'Yeah?'

'The antiques centre, how do I get in?'

'You don't. It's shut today. Come back tomorrow morning, it opens at ten.' And she trudged off into the snow.

Alexa walked up to the doors and peered through into the room beyond. It seemed like a junkshop with pretensions, a barely organised assembly of bits and pieces, crammed cheek by jowl in floor-to-ceiling cabinets. Shut. And the most unlikely of settings for a clandestine meeting with a demon lover. Perhaps Aidan Kane had a sense of humour after all.

She allowed herself a faint twinge of relief. But then she leant against the door and it yielded, swinging gently inwards. And like the fool that she was, Alexa stepped inside.

'Hello?' The door swung shut behind her, but there was no other sound to disturb the silence. She took a few steps forward into the mad museum. 'Anybody here?'

Nothing. Not even an echo.

She could have simply turned tail and gone home, but curiosity had already taken over. Her eyes were scanning the glass cabinets, picking out the beautiful and the grotesque: a Meissen teacup next to a model of Blackpool Tower; a tiny Georgian silver cream-jug sitting inside a cracked chamber-pot. The whole place was filled with that peculiar smell you always got in antique shops: beeswax polish and mildew, mixed with the faint aroma of instant coffee.

Since she was here anyway, surely there was no harm in looking. She knew she shouldn't be here, but if the owners were careless enough to leave the doors unlocked, why, you could hardly blame people for wandering in. Just think . . . if you wanted, you could steal anything that took your fancy. And there didn't even seem to be any security cameras to capture the wicked deed.

She walked through the ground-floor showroom and followed the stairs up to the first floor. Every inch that could conceivably be used was crammed with merchandise. On the first floor, she found a long corridor running the length of the building, lined with small square showrooms on either side. One was full to the brim with ephemera – old cornflake packets, advertisements for Strand cigarettes, music hall song sheets. Another held row upon row of Suzi Cooper and Clarice Cliff, whilst opposite a one-armed teddy bear sat lopsidedly on top of a 1930's radiogram.

It was all fascinating enough, of course, but there was nothing to be passionate about. Nothing you'd want to slip into your pocket and take home with you, hoping no one would notice it was missing.

Until she stepped into the last booth on the right, and saw it. Probably the most exquisite necklace she had ever set eyes on, a triple collar of freshwater pearls, set at its centre with a huge and lustrous emerald. The kind of jewellery that only a princess would wear. Opulent, sensual, and completely excessive.

Dare she touch it? She reached out and let her fingertips explore it, lingering, stroking, experiencing its cold smoothness. And then, on sudden impulse, she lifted it from its stand. It was just as she was raising it to her throat, to admire her reflection in the mirror, that she saw something sticking to the back of it, a tiny circular piece of paper which bore three words:

LOOK BEHIND YOU

With a gasp, she turned round, dropping the necklace to the floor in a clatter of pearls.

'You!'

Aidan Kane was leaning against the doorframe, arms folded, looking casually demonic in a black, Edwardian-style jacket, matching trousers and a silver brocade waistcoat.

'Take it, I chose it for you.'

He bent and picked up the necklace carefully, inspecting it with interest as he turned it over in his hands.

'You adore it, of course. I knew you would.'

Alexa stared at him, realisation filtering slowly into her consciousness.

'How . . . ? How did you . . . ?'

'How did I know what would please you?' He chuckled softly. 'How did I know that you have a taste for extravagance and decadence? That your aesthetic tastes are very different from your husband's? I have my methods. You don't need to know what they are.'

Alexa hardly knew whether to be angry or afraid.

'What is this all about?'

Aidan sighed.

'You're so impetuous, so . . . impatient. You want to *know* everything instead of simply *enjoying* it.'

'What is there to enjoy? You're blackmailing me, remember?'

'Such an ugly word from such a beautiful mouth.' Alexa flinched as Kane reached out and stroked the pearl collar against her cheek, but his touch was sensual, almost tender. 'You must learn to relax, Alexa. Didn't Miranda Ross teach you anything?'

'Don't touch me,' snapped Alexa, belatedly pulling herself together.

Aidan withdrew his long fingers slowly and sensually from her skin, leaving behind a faint shiver of regret.

'You have an extremely low opinion of me, Alexa.'

'What do you expect?'

'I expect you to use your mind as well as your senses. It's no use putting on the outraged virgin act, it won't wash with me. I've seen what you're really like, Alexa. Remember that.'

And how could she not remember? She loathed this man with every atom of her being, despised him for what he had brought her to – despised him even more than Piet, who had somehow cajoled her into taking part in this ridiculous and dangerous pantomime.

'Take it, Alexa.' Aidan offered her the jewel. 'I meant it when I said I chose it for you. And you want it, I can see it in your eyes.' You want me too, said the expression on Kane's face, but he was too much of a snake to just come out and say it.

Alexa pushed away the pearl collar. It jangled prettily in Aidan's fingers, with a flash of green fire as the emerald caught reflected light from the snow outside the windows.

'Don't flatter yourself, Mr Kane. I don't want anything from you.'

'All right then.' Kane's face relaxed. 'You can leave now if that's what you want.'

Alexa turned and stared at him.

'If . . . ?'

'You heard me, Alexa. You're free to go. Of course, I have the photographs and one day soon I may choose to call up Piet and show them to him . . .'

'What do you want?'

Kane stepped closer. She could smell the cool, lemony cologne on his skin, the sweetness of his breath.

'You know that.'

A frisson ran through Alexa. It wasn't fear, though it should have been. It was excitement.

'Why don't we walk round the centre?' said Kane, suddenly drawing away. 'You enjoy antiques?'

'Why don't you tell me? Since you seem to know everything about me.'

Kane chuckled as they walked back down the silent corridor towards the doors of the lift. A ballerina automaton watched with knowing eyes from the top of a nearby cabinet, one leg in the air, rouged lips parted, head cocked on one side as though about to make some ribald comment.

'Early English porcelain, Majolica ware, Deco silver . . . am I right?'

'You forgot about Fabergé eggs.'

'Ah yes. Your fantasy, to own something priceless. I wonder what other fantasies you have, Alexa.' Kane pressed the 'call lift' button, and Alexa heard the lift cables grating and squeaking somewhere up above.

'Where are we going?'

'To the top floor. There's something I want to show you.'

The lift arrived, a dirty little box with concertina doors you had to drag across yourself. As the inner door slid home, locking her inside with Kane, Alexa marvelled at her own madness.

'I must be crazy. I don't know anything about you, you could be a . . . a homicidal maniac.'

Her eyes met Kane's in the flickering orange light of a single guttering bulb.

'Yes, I could, couldn't I? Does that thought excite you, Alexa?'

'What do you mean?' There was a strange fluttering in the pit of Alexa's stomach, an ache that was travelling slowly down towards the hot, moist triangle between her thighs.

'Does it turn you on to think of the danger?'

'You're crazy,' she whispered.

But the ache wouldn't go away, no matter how she fought to banish it. She closed her eyes and turned her face away, but if anything it only intensified the sensations. She found herself concentrating on them, savouring the frantic thump of her heart and the sweet, pulsing ache which hung like a divine heaviness at the very base of her belly, coaxing the petals of her secret flower.

A slight jolt was followed by the ping of the lift bell. Kane's hand on her elbow guided her out onto the topmost floor of the old warehouse. More rows of retail units, a café, horrible cracked linoleum, a smell of mildewed books.

'Turn right,' said Kane, 'and walk to the very end.'

'But . . .'

'Past the escritoire – it's rather nice, isn't it? But overpriced; so few people know the value of anything any more.'

Alexa's fingers brushed the aged-smoothed walnut surface then she was walking on, slowly and mechanically, past cases of books and pictures of prize bulls in chipped stucco frames.

'Where are we going?' The end of the corridor loomed up ahead, dead and blind; going nowhere. A cul-de-sac bounded by piles of old books and heavy, country-house mahogany furniture that no one would ever buy. 'There's nothing . . .'

'Here. Do you see it?' Just before the very end of the passageway, Kane stopped her and turned her to gaze through the window of the very last unit. A Fabergé egg gazed back at her from the other side of the glass, encased in its own locked cabinet. 'Exquisite, no? Only a copy, of course, a poor imitation, but pleasing enough in its own small way.'

'It's wonderful,' murmured Alexa, lost in reflection as her gaze travelled over the intricacy of the workmanship, the tiny jewelled eggs lying on scarlet velvet within a shell of enamelled gold.

'Perhaps. But you can't escape the fact that it's a compromise,' said Kane. He was standing behind her, and she felt his hair brush her cheek as he bent to kiss the nape of her neck. 'A fake.'

'Please . . . don't . . .'

'A compromise,' repeated Kane. 'And I never accept compromises. I would accept any danger, rise to any challenge, but I would never accept anything less than everything. Neither should you.'

Alexa swung round. She wasn't sure what it was that filled her with sudden apprehension; perhaps a tensing of the muscles in Kane's hands, or some change in the rhythm of his breathing. She was going to tell him, 'I don't understand, I want to leave. Now.' But there was no time to say anything.

'No compromises, Alexa.' Out of the blue, Kane struck out with one booted foot, kicking at the old doors which had once been used for hauling in sacks of grain, or barrels of wine. The cheap padlock shattered and the doors flew open, letting in a miniature whirlwind of wind-driven snow.

'Step forward. Look down.'

'No!' squealed Alexa, but Kane was behind her and he was pushing her forward, out of the musty security of the warehouse and onto a tiny wooden platform, no more than three or four feet wide, which jutted out over a dazzling, dizzying, sickening drop.

'Look, Alexa. One hundred and eleven feet, six and a half inches. That's to the quayside. Of course, if you were to fall into the water . . .'

'Aidan!' It was the first time she'd called him by his first name, the first time the rawness of emotion had cut through the protective wall she had built around herself. 'Don't make me . . .'

But in a funny kind of way, she wanted him to make her. She wanted him to take her by the hand and lead her out onto that narrow, creaking platform; to make her balance perilously between heaven and hell and open herself to the terrifying adrenaline rush of complete, unblemished fear.

His body was hot and hard beneath the tight-fitting suit. She clung to him like a child, her fingers clawing at his back, her face upraised to his.

'Don't . . . make me . . . look down.'

He took her face between his hands and kissed it, forcing his lips against hers, his tongue pushing a few melting snowflakes into the warmth within. Gasping for breath, she found herself responding, her passion fire-hot though her fingers were white and frozen and her whole body shook with terror.

I want you, she thought. I'm scared and I hate you, but I still want you, I can't stop myself.

Kane's hands slid from her waist. His eyes bored into her, unforgiving, knowing everything.

'Now let go. And look down.'

She pleaded with him silently, but there was no escape. Painfully slowly, shaking with terror, she released her grip on him and, with eyes closed against the driving snow, turned to face the drop.

'Look, Alexa. Open your eyes. Then tell me that you have ever felt so alive in your whole life.'

With agonising slowness, she forced open her eyes and looked down, down, down, through the tumbling snowflakes to the dock beneath. So far, so unreal. If she took one step out into the empty air, she would fly; no, float down gently like a snowflake.

No. She would fall like a stone, be crushed on the dockside. She was paralysed, she couldn't move a muscle . . .

As vertigo struck and she swayed sideways, Aidan Kane caught hold of her and dragged her back into the warehouse. He did not speak. She clawed at him for a long, long time, until his warmth soaked into her and drove away the fear.

'Make love to me,' she whispered, gazing up into his face. 'Now.'

He smiled. 'No.'

And turning on his heel, he walked away.

Chapter 5

'Alexa. Alexa, where are you going?'

'What the hell is it to you?' snapped Alexa, pushing past Piet and heading upstairs. As she ran up the staircase she unbuttoned her coat and threw it off, kicking off her shoes, peeling off her gloves and letting them fall down the stairwell into the hall.

'Alexa . . .'

She heard Piet coming after her, and swung round, flinging the unused alarm down the stairs at him. Her hands were shaking, damn them, her whole body still fighting the angry ache of rejection.

'What?'

He reached out and touched her arm. She shook him off.

'I was worried about you.'

'Don't give me that!'

Piet's golden eyes pleaded with her to believe him, but she was angry as hell; even more with herself than she was with Piet, for she was the weak link in all of this, the pawn who'd allowed herself to be used . . . and then fallen into the trap of wanting the game to go on.

'It's true. I'm sorry, Alexa, I was wrong to ask you to . . .'

Piet paused. 'What happened?'

Alexa spat back the answer.

'Nothing.'

'*Nothing*?'

'*Absolutely* nothing. Are you satisfied now?'

She turned round and walked up the remaining three steps to the landing, her stockinged feet sinking into the deep pile of the stair-carpet. Warmth was coming back slowly to her, but the feeling of aching numbness had little to do with the biting January cold. Aidan had teased her, played with her, forced her into wanting him. And then, when he'd taken her to the screaming-point of desire, he'd rejected her, as good as turned round and laughed in her face. She loathed him. But her body still ached for him, and that made her hate him even more.

Piet followed her into the bedroom, where she flopped down onto the end of the bed. The cheval mirror by the window taunted her with the image of damp, dishevelled hair and smudged lipstick; and one pearl-drop earring, swinging forlornly against her cheek. She wondered if the other one was still lying on the cracked linoleum at the antiques centre, or had Aidan Kane picked it up and put it into his pocket, a souvenir of another game well-played?

'Go away,' she said, wearily rolling down one pale caramel stocking. But Piet slid onto the bed behind her and began stroking the tiny short hairs on the back of her neck.

'I really am sorry,' he repeated, making her shiver with light, coaxing finger-strokes that ran all the way down from the base of her hairline to the valley between her shoulder-blades.

'Don't,' she murmured softly. Not that she expected Piet to take any notice. And in a funny sort of way, even though she was angry with him for making her do his dirty work, she wanted him to do this. Every nerve-ending in her body had been over-stimulated to the point of physical pain. If she didn't find some way to satisfy the urge that Kane had awakened, she would surely go crazy.

Piet stopped stroking her neck and, kneeling behind her on the bed, slipped his arms round Alexa's waist. Without meaning to, she purred as his two hands slid slowly and deliberately upwards; cupping her breasts so lightly that they barely made contact, yet set the nipples tingling and burning.

'I really hate you, Piet.'

'I know.'

His lips touched her earlobe, kissing it, then taking it into his mouth. She felt his warm wetness engulf the flesh, his tongue winding about it, his teeth nibbling at it playfully. That was what made it so difficult to play hard to get with Piet; he knew all the little gestures that turned her on, the quirks and the caresses, the buttons that switched on her secret electricity.

'If you don't stop that . . .'

To her disappointment, he did stop. The warm kisses turned to a cold frisson as his lips drew away.

'You've lost an earring.'

'Have I?' She tried to sound casual, but she knew her voice was shaking.

'You know you have. Did he take it from you?'

'No.'

'He didn't . . . hurt you?'

79

Alexa raised her head until her eyes met Piet's in the mirror.

'How do you know he turned up at all?'

'But he did?' She felt Piet's hands tighten slightly about her breasts.

'I'm going to take a bath.' Gently but firmly she prised his hands away and slid off the bed.

Piet stood in the doorway as she turned on the taps and hot water roared into the double-sized bath.

'Are you ever going to forgive me?'

Alexa didn't reply. Resting her left foot on the edge of the bath, she rolled down her second stocking and peeled it off. Piet's eyes followed her hands hungrily, dwelled for a long time on the darkly shadowed portion of bare thigh beneath her short green skirt.

'Let me undress you. You look exhausted.'

She thought fleetingly of telling him to go to hell, but his hands felt warm and strong on her bare shoulders. She shrugged.

'Whatever.'

The zipper on her skirt swished softly down, and Piet eased it down over her thighs. His hands followed it down, lingering longer than they needed to on the rounded swell of her backside.

'You have the most glorious buttocks I have ever seen.'

'Yeah?'

She was facing away from him, and he couldn't see the small smile which flickered over Alexa's lips. She knew she looked good in suspenders and a white lace thong; hadn't she spent an hour dressing to please Aidan Kane? The smile faded. Dressing like some sacrificial victim – and when she'd offered herself to him on a plate, he'd turned her down.

Piet's fingers traced the deep cleavage which ran between Alexa's small, firm buttocks; not making any attempt to slip between but skating lightly over the flesh. Alexa felt the most acute pangs of excitement, suddenly realising that she was holding her breath, silently praying for the feel of his fingers pushing aside the thong, sliding inside her up to the hilt.

'Now the blouse, Alexa.' Piet's hands reached round and felt for the buttons, small and rather fiddly discs covered in white silk. They yielded so slowly that Alexa was tempted to help him. But that would have spoiled the game.

Cool white silk slid tantalisingly slowly over her shoulders, exposing the flesh beneath. Piet's lips travelled over the smooth skin, covering it with the very lightest of kisses, following the blouse with first one bra strap, then the other.

Alexa shivered as Piet released the catch on her bra and she felt the elastic spring silently apart. Her breasts seemed to sigh into his hands as the white satin bra fell, unheeded, into the swirling bathwater.

'And the most beautiful breasts,' purred Piet. 'The most beautiful breasts in the world.' He squeezed lightly, Alexa's nipples agreeably trapped between his fingers so that they were rubbed and pulled as Piet's fingers tightened about the two small, hard globes.

He was pressing hard against her and she felt his dick grinding urgently into the small of her back. Instinct drew her hand back to touch him, her fingernails scratching along the hard, fleshy baton to its sensitive tip.

'You gorgeous vixen . . .'

He sounded so like Aidan Kane that Alexa withdrew her fingers suddenly, spinning round in his arms so that they were face to face. She was panting, her lips moist with spittle, as Piet forced his mouth on hers and with his free hand, stripped down her pants and suspender belt.

She wriggled, her fingernails raking down Piet's flanks, then wrestling with the zipper on his trousers. But Piet took her hand and, releasing her from his kiss, pressed it to his lips.

'Not yet,' he said. 'First I'm going to bathe you.'

Alexa defied him with a pout of her smudged candy-pink lips.

'Who says I want you to?'

'Then what would you have me do?' Piet's eyes twinkled as he kissed her hand a second time. '*Mistress*?'

She thought for a moment.

'You'll do anything I want?'

'Anything.'

'Kiss my feet.'

Sliding down her body, he trailed kisses all the way down from the moist crease beneath her breasts to her navel, the mossy mound of her sex and the long, aching smoothness of her thighs. As he knelt there on the carpet in front of her, his blond head bent and his tongue caressing her bare toes, Alexa wanted to laugh with exhilaration. The tables were turned, she wasn't the pawn any more, Piet was her slave. It felt even better than she'd expected.

As Piet licked and sucked her toes, a warm and tingly

feeling climbed up her body, sending tiny electric shocks up her legs and through her belly to the epicentre of her sex. The warmth grew and intensified, until she felt so shaky and languid that her legs seemed too weak to hold her any longer. Slowly she lowered herself onto the edge of the bath, knees slightly apart. She looked down at Piet, his golden hair flopping forward over his face, his pink tongue lapping obediently between her toes.

'Higher,' she whispered. And his tongue began to climb and wind up from her toes to her heels, the backs of her ankles, the smooth muscle of her calves, her knees. 'Higher. Don't stop until I tell you to.'

Behind her, water crashed into the bath, spreading the scent of sweet almond oil all around her. Above and beyond it, Alexa could smell the scent of her own pussy, her own sacred oil, oozing fragrant and sweet from her hidden spring.

Piet's tongue crept up the inside of her thighs, lapping movements quickening and teasing as he grew closer and closer to her sex. Oh how she wanted to take his head between her hands and force it between her thighs, press his lips into the moist triangle of her sex and hold it there until he had satisfied the burning, incandescent need that throbbed through her swollen clitoris.

But she stopped him, a scant inch short of paradise.

'No more.'

Piet looked up at her, questioningly. His mouth and chin were wet with his own saliva. Alexa imagined her own juices running from his mouth, and almost climaxed at the thought of his tongue flicking lightly across her clitoris.

'But Alexa . . . I want to . . .'

Alexa shook her head reprovingly.

'If you want me to forgive you, you'll have to do what I want for a change.' Swinging her legs over the side of the bath, she plunged into the warm, foaming water and lay back, like Cleopatra in a lake of asses' milk. 'You can bathe me now.'

Piet laughed.

'And to think I was afraid of what might happen to you . . .' He took a cake of soap and lathered it, running his hand lightly over Alexa's throat and shoulder.

'Don't you want to know what did happen?' Alexa murmured her pleasure as the soapy hand circled her right breast, sweeping again and again over her erect and swollen nipple. 'Don't you want to know what I did with Aidan Kane?'

The hand on her breast stopped moving for a moment, then began again, a little harder this time, the fingers slightly bent so that the tips of the nails scratched the surface of Alexa's skin.

'Tell me.'

'At first, I thought he wasn't going to turn up. But he was one step ahead of me, inside the antiques centre, waiting for me. There was a necklace . . .'

'What kind of necklace?'

'Pearls and a huge emerald. He said it was a gift he'd chosen especially for me.' Eyes half closed, Alexa recalled the coldness of the pearls against her skin, the burning heat that had seemed to radiate from Aidan Kane's grey-green eyes.

'You took it?'

Alexa rolled over onto her belly in the bath, presenting her back and buttocks for Piet to caress.

'I threw it in his face.'

'And then?'

Alexa thought she heard Piet's breath quicken. His hand was moving down her back, circling lower and lower, now massaging soapy lather into her upraised buttocks as she half-lay, half-knelt in the bath.

'He started talking about antiques, and about knowing what I liked, better than I know myself. He took me up to the top floor of the centre. And then . . .'

She told Piet about the door at the end of the passageway, about the tiny wooden platform overlooking the quayside, and the freezing, biting snowflakes which had whirled and screamed around them as Kane dragged her out into the emptiness.

'For a split second,' she whispered. 'Just for a moment, I thought . . . I thought he was going to make me – right there on that platform . . .'

Piet's fingers slid down, smoothing the rich lather over Alexa's backside, teasing and insinuating it into the tight wet crease between her buttocks. She gasped as the tip of his index finger explored her anus, making it sting and contract at the harshness of the perfumed soap.

'Piet!'

'But he didn't? He didn't have sex with you at all?'

'No.'

'And you wanted him to? You wanted him to force you, is that it, Alexa?'

Alexa's heart was pounding in her chest. There was

something in Piet's voice, not jealousy or anger. Desire, that was it. She turned to look into his face and knew that he was sharing the selfsame excitement, the thrill of mad fantasy.

'Yes,' she whispered, curiously unashamed. 'I wanted him like crazy.'

'There, on the platform above the dock?'

'Yes. Yes, I wanted the danger almost as much as I wanted the sex. I wanted him to take me and fuck me and be the only thing preventing me from falling.'

'But it didn't happen.'

'All he wanted was the power, I see that now. He didn't want to fuck me, he got his kicks making me crazy for him.'

'Then he's the crazy one,' murmured Piet. 'Do you know how much you turn me on? Do you know how stiff my dick is for you?'

Without even bothering to undress, he slid into the bath, slopping foamy water over the side onto the new peach carpet. Alexa clawed his body hard against hers and tore down his zipper, reaching inside for the prize she craved.

'I was thinking about you,' gasped Piet. 'About you getting it on with Aidan Kane. Fantasising.'

'All the time he was kissing me and pawing me . . . I wanted him to have me while you watched.' Alexa's fingers curled about the stalk of Piet's dick and drew it between her legs. She lay back against the side of the bath and lifted her left thigh, curling it over Piet's right hip. 'Insane, isn't it? I don't even fancy him.'

'Not even a little?' Piet's voice coaxed as his hands seized Alexa's bum-cheeks and pulled her hard onto the spike of his cock. She knew what he wanted her to say, and it was easy because it wasn't even a lie.

'Well . . . maybe just a little.'

'I want you to tell me everything. What he felt like, where he touched you, what you wanted to do with him.'

'I wanted to do . . . everything. Anything he asked of me, I'd have done it there and then.'

'My little slut. My incredible little slut.'

They made fierce, uninhibited love right there in the bath, driven on by the power of their shared fantasy; each knowing that however exciting it might be, the game was only a game. For Aidan Kane had had his little bit of fun, his moment of complete control; so what more could he possibly want? And what had they to fear from a joker who got his kicks from power-games and then backed out at the last moment? As Piet commented later, as he smoothed warm aromatherapy oil into Alexa's breasts: 'I don't suppose you'll ever hear from him again.'

The funny thing about Aidan Kane was that, long after that snowy day at Gloucester Docks, his influence seemed to linger on.

Sex between Alexa and Piet had never been better. In fact, it was dynamite. In her heart of hearts, Alexa had to admit to herself that before the conference at Boroughbridge Hall, their sex-life had been if not boring, then perhaps a little lacking in spice. But since Aidan Kane had invited himself into their lives, things had been very, very different. It was as though something invisible had happened, as though a switch had been tripped and Piet and Alexa had rediscovered all the energies and appetites of the days when they first met.

Days passed. Then days turned into weeks. If Alexa sometimes thought about Aidan Kane, and maybe even fantasised about him in the darkness of her own dreams, she never felt the need to say so. And in any case, SuccessWorks was taking up more and more of her time, with Damian taking on increasingly prestigious contracts and delegating as much as he could get away with to other members of the agency staff.

One morning in February, Alexa arrived early in the office in the hope of finishing off some roughs before the phone started ringing. But she had hardly switched on her PC when a head appeared round the door of her office. It was Sonia, Damian's PA.

'Hi, Alexa. Damian says can he see you in his office in five minutes.'

Oh God what now, thought Alexa. Damian Goldstone was getting distinctly neurotic in his old age – and he was only thirty-two. Still, twenty-two was middle-aged in this high-pressure business.

'What's it about?'

Sonia shrugged and shook her head.

'Search me. But he's just asked me for black coffee and indigestion tablets.'

Alexa climbed the stairs to Damian's office, wondering what it was she was supposed to have done wrong this time. Last week it was an argument about the precise shade of yellow to make a plastic promotional daffodil. The week before that it had been some company director complaining that the photograph on his publicity leaflets made him look like Mussolini – which, seeing as he was fat, bald and Italian, was perhaps not that surprising.

The door of Damian's office was ajar but she knocked anyway. One time she'd barged straight in and found him 'in conference' without his trousers on.

'Yeah?'

She stepped inside.

'Sonia said you wanted to see me.'

'Oh, right. Sit down. I'll be with you in a minute.' Damian swivelled his chair round and, telephone tucked under his chin, barked out a few orders while tapping frantically into his computer. 'Four forty-two. No, forty-*two*. I'll get back to you later, OK?'

Slamming the phone down, he swivelled back to face Alexa. His usually floppy ginger hair was ruffled up on one side from jamming the telephone receiver to his ear, and he looked more like a freckle-faced schoolboy than ever.

'I've got a job for you.'

'Another one? You said you wanted the roughs for Paradise Hotels by five o'clock today . . .'

'Get Siobhan to help, she spends all day on her backside anyway, do her good to do a bit of work for a change. Anyhow, this is for tomorrow, not today. Coffee?'

Alexa peered at the swamp-black concoction in the bottom of Damian's cup and shook her head.

'Thanks but no thanks.' She drew up a chair and sat down. 'So what is it this time?'

'I'm about to take on another important client.'

'We don't have the staff to take on any more clients, Damian!'

The schoolboy expression hardened, ageing Damian a good ten years in the process.

'That's for me to judge. But you know the first rule of business: grow or die. This agency is going to expand if I have to attach it to a foot-pump and blow it up myself.' Rummaging in a drawer he took out a business card and shoved it across the desk. 'I want you to go and see this guy tomorrow.'

Alexa glanced down at the card. '"Arcadia Holdings, David Protheroe, Director." What do they do?'

'That's what you're going to find out. The important thing is that they want us to design a PR campaign for them. If they're satisfied that we can give them what they want. Which,' he added, looking Alexa straight in the eye, 'they of course will be.'

'So why me?'

'Let me put it this way. The guy is – how shall I put it – a touch difficult. He's going to require careful handling.'

Light was dawning. Damian was dumping on her for the umpteenth time.

'You mean he's a complete bastard and you think I can get round him.'

'If you like. The fact is, Alexa, I sent you on that management training course precisely so that you could improve your communication skills and deputise for me whenever necessary. Have you any idea how much that bloody conference cost? I fully intend getting my money's worth out of you, Alexa.'

'But I'm a graphic design specialist! I design leaflets and plastic daffodils . . .'

'You're part of *my* public relations consultancy, Alexa, and that means that you do what I tell you to do. And I'm telling you to go to Swindon tomorrow and do whatever you have to do to get this account.'

Alexa picked up the business card and pushed it into her pocket. She managed a sarcastic laugh.

'There are one or two things I wouldn't do, even for you, Damian.'

Damian looked back at her with steady self-assurance.

'Oh no there aren't,' he replied. And he meant it.

Swindon had never been one of Alexa's favourite places. Come to think of it, she was hard-pressed to imagine it being anyone's favourite place. Tower-blocks, a soullessly symmetrical shopping mall and dreary redbrick terraces made it precisely the kind of town that needed a good PR job.

As she drove along, Alexa wondered about David Protheroe and Arcadia Holdings. What was it that was so 'difficult' about him? And why did he need SuccessWorks to give his company a new image? Damian had been annoyingly vague in briefing her for this meeting. Dammit, she didn't even know what kind of business Arcadia Holdings was involved in – and she had the distinct impression that Damian didn't know much more. Consequently she'd done hardly any preparation. If she wasn't careful she was going to look like an incompetent amateur.

Still, at least she was dressed to kill. For a banking consultant, Piet de Maas had an excellent eye for couture.

This mauve Escada suit with matching shoes, sleeveless white lace body and a simple white-gold necklace set with amethysts had been a present from Piet. Together, they managed to combine a businesslike elegance with a teasingly voluptuous sensuality. Underneath the body she was wearing a sheer skintone bra, which gave the overall effect of naked flesh, peeping coquettishly through the open weave of the lace. For a final touch she had twisted her hair up into a loose plait, leaving a few silky curls to spiral softly at the back of her neck.

'Old Swindon', that's what it said on the business card. Alexa didn't even realise there *was* such a thing as an old Swindon, just bits that were slightly less brassily new than the rest.

But Old Swindon turned out to be quite a surprise: the Wimbledon Village of Swindon, set aside from the rest of the town and consisting of three or four intersecting streets of smart shops and expensive restaurants. Designer furnishing fabrics, antiques, recherché couture clothes and quirky little brasseries rubbed shoulders with a bicycle repair shop and an ivy-clad coaching inn. Not a Pizza Hut in sight. Things were looking up.

Taking her briefcase from the passenger seat, Alexa slid out of the car. She glanced at her reflection in the window of the wine shop, easing her jacket down over her hips. It was very cold, the air dry and crisp with unmelted frost even though it was almost lunchtime. She glanced at the card again. Number thirty-four . . .

But number thirty-four was a second-hand bookshop, a bay-windowed shambles of jumbled paperbacks and old copies of the *Boy's Own Paper*. There had to be some mistake. Alexa walked up to the door and pushed it open, stepping into a warm fustiness which caught in the back of her throat. A middle-aged man was halfway up a ladder, reaching down a dusty volume from the top shelf.

'Here you are, Mrs Williams. The fourth edition, there's only one plate missing.'

The woman in grey shook her head and waved the book aside.

'It has to be the first edition, or not at all.'

With a shrug, the man on the ladder replaced the book on the shelf and jumped down, wiping his hands on his trousers.

'Sorry, no can do.'

Alexa cut in.

'Excuse me . . .'

'Can I help you?'

'I hope so. Is this Arcadia Holdings?'

'Nope.'

Alexa's heart sank.

'I'm looking for a Mr David Protheroe?' She took the business card out of her pocket.

'Oh. Right.' The middle-aged man pointed to the far-distant rear of the shop, lost in the dusty twilight between the top-heavy stacks of books. 'You want Rare Books. Down the stairs to the basement, there's a door at the far end.'

'Thanks.' For nothing, Alexa added under her breath, picking her way between the over-crammed shelves, past innumerable bound copies of *Punch* and dust-covered heaps of yellowing magazines. If this was Mr Protheroe's business empire, it was going to take more than a free plastic daffodil to resurrect its image.

She walked slowly and gingerly down the badly-lit steps which led between whitewashed walls into the basement. Everything smelt of damp, and she wondered why she'd bothered dressing up. When she got back to Cirencester, she'd give Damian a piece of her mind.

The door at the far end of the basement room was marked: 'RARE AND ANTIQUARIAN BOOKS.' On the wall beside the door was the keypad for a combination lock.

She tried the handle. It turned but the door was locked. She knocked. In the echoing, uneasy silence she heard the sounds of voices and shuffling feet drifting down from the shop above. She knocked again. Perhaps he wasn't there. She'd give him ten more seconds and, if he hadn't turned up by then . . .

A metallic click sounded, and a green light flashed on above the lock. The door was unlocked. She pulled herself together and turned the handle.

'Hello? Mr Protheroe . . .'

But there was no one there. What's more, the room she stepped into wasn't some dingy cellar filled with mildewed books no one wanted to read. It was cool, dry, lined from carpeted floor to moulded ceiling with locked bookcases, and filled with flat glass-topped cases covered with squares of black velvet.

Her eyes ran over the glass cases and the Deco reading lamps, the gilded leather bindings and the marble statuette of Minerva. Well, well, well. Maybe she'd misjudged this Protheroe character after all. This was no two-bit secondhand shop, it was more like one of the reading rooms at the British Library.

Then she heard footsteps and swung round. He was standing behind her, in the doorway; expensively trendy in Ralph Lauren but still every inch the Prince of Darkness.

Not David Protheroe at all. Aidan. Aidan Kane.

Alexa's skin prickled, the hairs bristling on the back of her neck as a frisson of delicious terror ran cold fingers all over her body. Her mouth opened, but she couldn't think of a single thing to say and her throat felt absurdly constricted.

Kane stepped into the room, closing the door behind him with a soft click. The tiny red light flicked back on. Locked. No escaping now.

'So tell me, Alexa.' His smile was deliciously chilled, bittersweet as espresso coffee poured over vanilla ice cream. 'Did you miss me?'

Chapter 6

'Do you like the feel of leather, Alexa?'

Alexa stared back at Aidan Kane – or should that be David Protheroe? Head inclined to one side, he dared her to reveal her deepest secrets. Dared her with those eyes that seemed to demand so much . . . and know everything.

'W-why?'

'Oh, I just wondered.' Kane ran his fingers up the spine of a green Morocco-bound book. The title wasn't lost on Alexa: it was *120 Days of Sodom*. 'Perhaps you prefer PVC. Or rubber.'

'What *is* this?' demanded Alexa, breaking the spell and pushing the book away. 'You drag me here on false pretences, you even involve my boss in this stupid charade . . .'

'Would you have preferred it if I'd turned up at your office with a collar and leash and called you to heel, like the dear little mongrel bitch you are?'

'How dare you . . .'

Kane snapped his fingers. 'Heel, bitch.'

'Shut up. Shut *up*!'

She practically screamed into his face but Kane scarcely reacted, merely resting his hands on her shoulders and pinning

97

her arms to her sides with frightening ease.

'Let me go.'

'Only if you promise not to scratch my eyes out.'

'Why should I promise you anything?'

'Because, because if you don't, I'll tell Piet about your little indiscretion?'

Alexa almost spat back that she didn't give a damn what he told Piet, since Piet knew everything anyway. But, for some reason she couldn't quite fathom, she kept her mouth shut.

'Because if you don't, I might refuse to make love to you again?'

That hit home, with stinging intensity. Alexa shook herself free and turned her back on Kane, using anger to veil her own embarrassment and humiliation. The surge of excitement, too; the panting hunger that made her breasts ache within the soft cups of her bra.

'Why did you bring me here?' she demanded without turning round. 'And what the hell is Arcadia Holdings?'

'That's not important. A mere device.' Kane slid his hands round Alexa's waist and she could have wept with unwilling pleasure as his fingers slipped down over her belly, lightly skimming the mound of her sex through the unforgiving tightness of her skirt. His lips brushed her cheek as he whispered softly in her ear. 'Did you wear these clothes for me, Alexa?'

'I wore them for somebody called David Protheroe,' replied Alexa coldly. 'And in case you're wondering, Piet chose them for me.'

Kane chuckled. His fingers flicked open the buttons of

Alexa's jacket and slipped inside. Half-heartedly she pushed his hand aside but it slid straight back to its target, the hard-tipped cone of her right breast.

'So he dresses you up and sends you out to seduce other men. How very interesting.'

At this, Alexa kicked out furiously and tore free of Kane's embrace.

'Are you going to tell me why you've brought me here, or not? Because if not, I'm leaving. Now.'

'Not unless I choose to unlock that door. Until then, I'm afraid you're trapped in here with me.'

Alexa's heart pounded. What if Kane was some kind of maniac, what if . . . ? She fought to keep calm.

'If you don't unlock it right now, I'll scream the place down.'

'If you must. But no one will hear you, this room is extremely well sound-proofed. I designed it myself.'

'OK. If that's what you want.' Alexa walked across to the nearest bookcase and seized the first thing that came to hand – a collector's edition of Ronsard, whose jewel-encrusted cover sat heavy in her hand. She raised her arm behind her head, imagining the satisfying thud as it hit the wall. Go on, stop me, she willed Kane. Show fear, surprise, anything.

But Kane just shook his head and, turning away, gently slid away the velvet cover on one of the glass-topped cases.

'You wouldn't destroy anything so beautiful,' he said. 'Come here and look at this.' He beckoned her across and, like the fool that she was, Alexa went. 'See how wonderfully well it's painted. Don't you think the penis is a masterpiece of erotic observation?'

She looked down into the glass case. There, on a bed of red silk, lay a medieval illuminated book, open at a picture of two lovers on the ramparts of a castle. The woman, her gown ruched up about her waist, was bending forward, displaying two fine and rounded buttocks; her beau preparing to plunge his huge, curving cock deep into her hungry arse. There were other people in the gardens below, yet the lovers seemed not to care who might see them taking their pleasure. In spite of herself, Alexa couldn't tear her eyes away.

'It's . . . interesting,' she said, managing somehow to conceal the throb of lust between her thighs.

'See how the artist exaggerates the size of the glans and the testicles?' Kane's voice soothed, almost hypnotically, his finger tracing patterns on the glass above the picture. 'It makes you wonder if the poor girl's anus could possibly stretch far enough.'

Alexa followed his fingertip, her mouth dry, her pulse racing. The painted dick seemed obscenely huge, its target tiny, scarcely more than a brownish-pink dot between the girl's white buttocks. Without meaning to, she found herself imagining that she was the girl and Kane her hugely-endowed lover, his hands hot on her backside as he opened her up and prepared to plunge deep into her secret pleasure . . .

'I see I chose well,' commented Kane, sliding the velvet cover back over the case and picking up the copy of Ronsard from the carpet where it had slipped from Alexa's fingers. 'Oh Alexa, you really must learn to trust me. Completely. Until you do, you will never experience your body's full potential. You must believe that I know what is best for you.'

'Where are we going?' demanded Alexa as she struggled to keep up with Kane's long strides. She was cold and shivering, her nipples ice-hard underneath the flimsy white lace top and the thin mauve jacket.

'Does it matter?'

It was a good question. Perhaps it didn't matter. She had as good as abandoned herself to whatever Aidan Kane had planned for her, what did it matter where he was taking her?

'Tell me.'

'Looking for pleasure.'

'I don't understand.'

'"Looking for pleasure" – it's the title of a new exhibition on voyeurism in silent film. I think you'll find it . . . stimulating. Ah, here we are, the Arcadia Gallery. I've arranged for us to attend a private viewing.'

Alexa looked at Kane sharply.

'The *Arcadia* Gallery? Does that mean . . . ?'

But she could tell that Kane wasn't about to answer.

'This used to be a Primitive Methodist chapel,' he commented as they walked up the path to the front porch. 'About ten years ago it was deconsecrated and converted into a private gallery, specialising in film. As you know, I have a special interest in film.'

Images flashed into Alexa's mind. Suki's tongue flicking in and out of her pussy, her own mouth opening in ecstasy as Suki fucked her with a curled fist, ramming it in and out of her until her back arched and she screamed her pleasure out loud.

'You mean, an interest in filming innocent people and then blackmailing them,' she said drily.

'Oh no, Alexa. You were never, ever innocent.'

The gallery was quite busy for a weekday afternoon, affluent women in hats mingling with men in suits who had the despairingly hungry look of high-class salesmen, and a couple of arty-scruffy types who probably bought their clothes ready-torn from Harrods. A waitress in black and white striped dungarees was wandering about with a tray of drinks, but no one was taking very much notice of her.

You could see that the building had once been a chapel, though the architect had really gone to town on it. A staircase of white wrought iron led up in an irregular spiral, disappearing through a large circular hole in the middle of the first floor, through which Alexa glimpsed the rich reds and blues of a stained-glass fanlight. On the ground floor, the walls and floor were white, the dazzle broken up by the exhibits and by occasional screens, false walls and draperies in swathes of primary colour.

'Welcome to "Looking for pleasure",' smiled the girl in dungarees. 'Pioneers of silent film are to your right, modern silents are on the first floor and the pornographic images are in the annexe. Just ask if you need any help.'

Alexa was already wandering about, gazing at stills from early Meliès films and a series of images from a 'What the Butler Saw' machine, showing a voluptuous parlour-maid undressing as the butler watched through the keyhole. Her waist was encased in whaleboned stays, laced to no more than a couple of hands' span; and this made her big, soft breasts and large, doughy buttocks seem huge and almost cartoon-like.

'She knows he's watching her,' said Kane. 'Look how she's lifting her foot onto that chair, so he can see between her legs. She *wants* him to desire her.'

'Maybe that's just wishful thinking,' said Alexa coolly, though the parlourmaid's wickedly sensual smile was by no means lost on her; and the dark bush of her pubic hair revealed indecently moist folds of flesh, pouting provocatively from between plump outer labia.

'You know something? I like to watch,' said Kane's voice, softly conspiratorial in her ear. 'And I know how you love to be watched.'

She moved away from him, cheeks burning, trying to look as if she wasn't with him. But as she turned right, past a life-size statue of Valentino as the Sheikh and a papier-mâché screen inlaid with mother-of-pearl nudes and pierced by tiny keyholes, she walked straight into the annexe.

Quite simply, she'd never seen anything quite like it. On the whole of the opposite wall, a scene from a recently-discovered Mary Pickford film was being projected in a never-ending tape-loop. The ingénue heroine was sitting in front of a dressing-table, wearing nothing but her nightgown and brushing her long hair. When the bedroom door opened and a dark stranger sprang onto her, stripping the chaste nightdress from her breasts, she cried out in silent astonishment and fear. When he threw her onto the bed, pulled down her drawers and scythed his cock into her in a single, savage thrust, she wriggled and writhed, and her eyes grew large in utter amazement. And it happened again and again and again.

'You see,' said Kane, coming up beside Alexa.

'See what?'

'It happens again and again. And every time she is completely astonished. She never sees what is going to happen to her.'

'How could she!' protested Alexa.

'But he knows. He's been watching her. He knows everything about her. And he knows how much pleasure they're going to share when he fucks her. Because every time is the first time.'

He touched Alexa's arm and as she half-turned towards him, her jacket fell open, revealing the shamelessness of her swollen breasts, the tiny pouting tongues of her nipples, so hard and protuberant beneath the lacy body.

'The first time', he repeated, giving each word significance. Then, 'Shall we take a look through there? I believe there are some interesting modern works.'

Drawn on by terrible kind of lustful fascination, Alexa walked past a group of chattering women discussing the dimensions of a Mapplethorpe penis, and into a kind of side-room where the lighting was more subdued and all the exhibits were snippets of film, screened in wall-mounted frames which made them look like animated paintings.

In *Sixty Second Orgasm*, a series of stills taken at one-second intervals had been strung together to produce a jerky film of two men enjoying oral sex; ending with a rather beautiful come-shot showing glossy white semen dripping down over closed eyelids. On a free-standing wall in the centre of the room, five screens had been placed side by side, each one showing a different person masturbating while watching a pornographic film on television.

Overlaying the moving images were captions in irregular white lettering. 'C'MON BABY, LIGHT MY FIRE' straggled across the face of a masked leatherboy, kneeling with his hands chained behind his back and his pretty, pierced dick jerking back and forth between the strings of an electric guitar. 'EXQUISITE CORPSE' dripped wetly over the oiled nakedness of a squirming girl, rubbing her pussy hard on the lid of a brass-handled coffin. And on the third screen, 'BREAD AND CIRCUSES', a middle-aged woman in dowdy clothes was sitting on a sofa, watching some pornographic foreign quiz-show while bringing herself off with the wooden handle of her broom.

'How do you get your kicks, Alexa?' enquired Kane, folding his arms and standing back to get the benefit of all five screens at once.

'I thought you knew everything about me,' replied Alexa archly. 'You don't need me to tell you that.'

'Perhaps not. But maybe I get my kicks in hearing you tell me how you get yours.'

Alexa knew she could just turn round and walk away, leave this grotesque place, get in her car and drive off back to Cirencester. But something was holding her back. The images had got inside her head, and her body was rebelling against her determination to despise and reject Aidan Kane. He was standing very close to her, close enough to reach out and touch her . . .

Staring at the screens, she imagined herself naked and oiled like the girl on the coffin, only it wasn't cold smooth oak between her thighs but Aidan Kane's hard, lean body;

not a brass handle nudging into the wet triangle of her sex, but Kane's eager dick. Was it huge and hard and thick; was it slender and curved and sharp as a lance? She imagined curling her fingers about it, stroking, squeezing, pumping, licking . . .

You're crazy, Alexa, she told herself. Crazy. This man – he's a stranger, he treats you like a toy, you don't even like him. And yet . . . and yet you want him more than anything else you can think of . . .

When Kane's hand closed on her shoulder, she started and let out an 'oh' of alarm.

'Shh.' Kane put his finger to his lips, shaking his head.

'What?'

Taking her hand he drew her behind one of the blood-red velvet drapes which screened a corner of the theatre.

'Better not make too much noise. Or do you *want* everyone to know?'

Behind the drape, they were screened from most of the theatre, except for a small section to the left of the central video-wall. At least, they might be screened from sight – but not from anyone who might care to eavesdrop. There were people moving about all over the place, talking, arguing points of artistic criticism, making nervous jokes about the kinds of things they'd rarely seen outside the grainy world of third-generation porn videos.

Alexa turned slowly to face Kane. It was dark behind the drape, and she could hardly make out more than his silhouette in the semi-darkness. His scent was unmistakable though, a musky blend of Acqua di Giò and something more subtle, more primeval. She breathed it in and shivered, the lace-edged satin of her panties suddenly uncomfortably constricting, pressing wickedly into the yielding softness of her sex.

There was no escaping it, the need for pleasure. Her clitoris was growing and swelling, pouting out of its fleshy hood like a panting tongue. Her nipples throbbed and tingled, her whole body felt tense, expectant, aching with unsatisfied need.

'Well?' said Kane softly. 'Have you seen enough, or would you like to see more?'

If she had half expected Kane to tear her clothes off, throw her against the wall and fuck her, Alexa was to be disappointed. He made no move, just stood there. Waiting. They both knew it was going to be Alexa who took that first, inexorable step.

Somebody switched on the sound system, and Diamanda Galas shrieked out like a rutting banshee, her unearthly voice as raw and primitive as sex itself. Closing her eyes, Alexa reached out and touched Kane's chest. A kind of wicked electricity shot through her, and she had to fight the urge to tear at his shirt, ripping and kissing and biting the flesh beneath. She could feel his heart beating, quite slowly and calmly; his flesh warm and hard with muscle. He didn't even flinch as her fingers curved into claws, her nails raking down his stomach to his trouser-buckle.

What are you doing? demanded a voice inside Alexa's head. But she knew perfectly well what she was doing, they both did. For the first time in as long as she could remember, Alexa was taking exactly what she wanted.

Holding her breath, she unfastened Aidan's belt and slid

down his zip, half-convinced that the soft swish would give them away and the curtain would be whisked aside, revealing her guilty hunger to the whole gallery. But nothing happened. Only the delicious travel downwards of the zipper-tag, and the incredible exhilaration of sliding her hand inside, feeling for his cock, shuddering with need as her fingers met a smooth rod of naked flesh, perfectly bare beneath his chinos.

Kane's dick tensed and arched slightly as Alexa's fingers curled about it, then she felt him relax again. Exploring him by touch alone, she let her fingers travel up and down the curving shaft, feeling the regular pulse of a fat vein on its underside, skimming the glassy wetness on the glans and smearing it on her palm so that it lubricated his whole cock.

And what now, Alexa? Kane did not speak, but she could hear his voice inside her head. What are you going to do now? How far will you dare go? Through the gap in the curtain, Alexa could just see the far end of the video wall, and the last screen, on which a woman was sitting on a carved oak chair, legs splayed wide and skirts up round her waist, masturbating herself with a fat tallow candle which dripped and glistened with her juices. 'THE BAWDY HAND IS ON THE PRICK OF MIDNIGHT,' declared the white letters that zig-zagged down over her low-cut bodice, picking out the glistening beads of sweat on her heaving breasts.

'It may be sexually stimulating,' said a woman's disapproving voice, on the other side of the velvet curtain. 'But is it art?'

Alexa was so close to Kane that she could smell him, breathe in the appetising tang of his sex. She had to have more, had to taste him, eat him, drink him. Sliding down his body, she ran a trail of open-mouthed kisses from his chest to his belly and then, no longer able to contain herself, parted her lips wide and circled the tip of Kane's dick.

His juice was salty and smooth on her tongue. The more she tasted, the more she had to have. She slid her fingers down to cup the heavy fruits of his balls, squeezing and scratching as she bore down on his dick, suddenly ravenous to have the full length of him inside her.

Kane shivered slightly as she took him deep into her mouth, so that his glans pressed against the back of her throat. A sense of erotic power filled Alexa. For the first time, she began to wonder just exactly who was in charge of this sexy pantomime. Perhaps Kane needed her sex as much as she needed his. She sucked hard on his glans and his cock twitched, a slippery ooze of lubricant dripping onto her tongue.

Then, just when Alexa thought she had him at her mercy, he pulled back – so suddenly that she almost cried out in protest. She felt empty, betrayed, cheated of her pleasure. Her clitoris throbbed, her labia dripped with frustrated excitement, soaking the crotch of her briefs. The taste of him lingered on her tongue, filling her with a desperate need for more, more, more.

With sudden, delicious savagery, Kane scooped her up in his arms; seizing her by the hips and lifting her up, he hooked her legs around his waist and forced his lips against hers. She growled with pleasure, moaning into his mouth as his tongue possessed her, thrusting between her lips, sharing the taste of his excitement. Over his shoulder, the same, mesmerising pictures rolled again and again, the candle disappearing into the girl's sex only to re-emerge and plunge back inside.

Pale, flickering shadows ran over Kane's silhouetted face as he slid one hand under Alexa's backside, eased up her skirt and pushed aside the crotch of her panties and the white lace bodysuit. Alexa could not suppress a little, sobbing cry of joy as he pushed her down hard onto his penis, forcing it up inside her, impaling her on the spike of their mutual desire. But Diamanda's unearthly soprano rose to a gothic wail, concealing this one, shameful sign of Alexa's weakness.

And in all honesty, at the moment when Alexa's hunger blossomed into a huge, all-consuming orgasm, she couldn't have cared less who knew what they were doing behind the blood-red curtain.

After her 'business meeting' with Kane, Alexa drove straight home. There seemed little point in going back to the office, and in any case, she needed time to think up some answers to the difficult questions Damian was bound to ask.

She reached home just after five. Her pulse quickened slightly as she saw Piet's car parked in the drive; she'd hoped for a chance of a bath and a glass of wine before he got home. Time to collect her thoughts . . .

'That you, Alexa?' His voice called down to her from the mezzanine where he'd installed his high-tech home office.

'Uh-huh.' She glanced in the hall mirror, readjusted her hair, hoped her make-up didn't look too smudged.

'You're early.'

'Oh, you know. The meeting ran on late, I thought I'd come straight home.'

'Why don't you come on up? I've just opened a bottle of Margaux.'

She threw off her coat and climbed the stairs to Piet's office. He was lounging in front of his PC in his dressing-gown, with a glass of red wine in his hand.

'Good day?' he asked.

In the two-second pause before she answered, Alexa almost told him everything. About Arcadia Holdings, about David Protheroe who had turned out to be Aidan Kane, and about what they had got up to at the gallery . . . But she didn't. She realised, to her surprise, that this was a secret she wanted to keep for herself, to enjoy, to gloat over, to take guilty pleasure in in the secrecy of her own thoughts. She wondered why.

'Not bad.' Alexa poured herself a glass of wine, leaned over and kissed Piet. Could he smell the lingering fragrance of Kane's dick, the mingled scents of sweat and semen and pussy-nectar? 'How about you?'

'I've just sold my interest in RYG.'

'Who?'

'RYG, it's a little tin mine in Malaysia.'

Alexa wrinkled her nose.

'Fascinating.'

'Actually, it is.' Piet ran his hand through his wavy golden hair. He looked, thought Alexa, just like the Alpha male in a pride of lions. And she found herself wanting him, with a passionate violence which quite astonished her. 'It's a competitive industry, and a bigger mine will buy it up in a few days or weeks.'

'And then?'

'It'll be closed down, to ruin the people who used to run it. Dozens of people will have their lives destroyed: workers, workers' wives, investors, investors' families . . .'

Alexa stared at Piet, horrified.

'But that's . . . that's awful!'

Piet shrugged.

'I know.' He fiddled with the mouse and clicked 'OFF'. 'But it's all about control. You see, we control the world around us to make our lives better . . .'

'You sound just like . . .' She stopped abruptly and Piet looked up.

'Like what?'

'Oh, nothing.' Just like Aidan Kane, she thought with a sudden shiver of realisation. 'Go on.'

'And we have to be ruthless, Alexa, because if we slip up for one moment, just one, someone else will step in and control the world for us.'

The following morning, after a long night of particularly hot sex, Piet left early for a meeting in Brussels. Alexa didn't hang around, she had work to do.

She took time to choose exactly the right outfit; the calf-length black suit with the thigh-split skirt, fake Tibetan lamb collar and cuffs, the one that Damian could never take his eyes off. Teamed with high-heeled black ankle boots and a leopard-print scarf, the ensemble gave the overall impression of a sleek, hungry cat on the prowl.

Growl, thought Alexa, touching up her lipstick and blowing herself a kiss in the mirror. Today she wasn't in the mood to take any shit from anyone.

Once she got to SuccessWorks, she didn't bother waiting for Damian to summon her to the inner sanctum for a debriefing. She simply swanned past the receptionist, took the lift to the fifth floor and stalked along the corridor to Damian's office.

The door was ajar. Inside, Damian was giving dictation to Sonia, that particularly fluffy-headed seventeen-year-old he laughingly referred to as his secretary.

'Was that a full stop, Mr Goldstone?'

'Full stop, complimentary close. Now why don't you come here and let me check your shorthand?'

The sound of a light slap was followed by girlish giggling.

'Oh, Mr Goldstone!'

'Come here, you bad girl . . .'

Alexa pushed open the door and strode in. Damian had Sonia over the desk, her pert bottom waggling in the air and his hand raised to administer a schoolmasterly slap. Two red faces jerked round to stare at Alexa as she burst through the door.

'Well, well, well. Staff training day is it, Damian?'

Damian couldn't have sprung back faster if his cock had been plugged into the mains.

'Alexa – what the hell do you think you're doing in here?'

'Waiting to have words with you. So why don't you send Sonia back to kindergarten and we'll talk?'

Sonia slid self-consciously off the desk, tugged her microskirt down over an extra half-inch of buttock, and edged towards the door.

'Shall I, er . . . ?'

'Go and type it up, I'll check it over later.' Damian waited for the door to close, then squared up to Alexa. 'What the bloody hell do you mean by barging in here?'

Alexa peeled off her gloves and tossed them onto Damian's desk. It really turned her on to see the way his eyes followed her every movement, almost popped out of their sockets as she perched on the edge of his desk, crossed her legs and undid the top button of her jacket.

'You're a bastard, Damian.'

'What!'

'I said, you're a bastard. That Protheroe guy . . .'

'What about him?'

'He was a complete time-waster – but you knew that already, didn't you? Some kind of joke was it, sending me all the way to Swindon?'

From the look on Damian's face, it was obvious that it was nothing of the sort. He looked completely gobsmacked. But Alexa was enjoying the game, revelling in this chance to make Damian feel distinctly uncomfortable.

'What are you on about, Alexa?' Damian was on the defensive now, shrinking back in his executive chair.

'Not quite with me yet? OK, let me spell it out.' She leaned forward, threatening Damian with the promise of her cleavage. God, but it felt good to have him mesmerised like this, hanging on her every word, practically drooling with the joy of subservience. 'He had no intention of placing an account with us, he just wanted the chance to grope a woman in a short skirt.'

'Come off it, Alexa . . .' he said weakly. But Alexa had his jugular between her teeth, and she was thirsty for the spurt of blood. 'Listen to me—'

'No, *you* listen to *me*. I'm sick of being treated like dirt. You think you can send me to the ends of the earth on some kind of wild-goose chase and I won't dare complain.'

'It's not like that.'

'Well I've had it with that, Damian. In fact, I've had it with SuccessWorks. And if you don't stop fucking me about and start treating me like a human being . . .'

'Alexa!'

'. . . I'm going to resign!'

Damian stared back at her, round-eyed.

'You don't mean that.'

'Oh yes I do.'

'You've . . . er . . . changed.'

Damian's breathing was rapid and shallow, and Alexa realised to her satisfaction that this was exciting him. So, Damian, she thought. I was right. Deep down, all you really want is for some fur-clad dominatrix to walk over your bare body in spike-heeled boots.

'Maybe. But I meant what I said.'

'This agency needs you, Alexa.' He was almost pleading now, eyes wide and practically panting as he gazed up at her.

'I know.' Alexa smiled thinly. 'Which is precisely why you're going to beg me to stay. And when you've done, you're going to beg me some more.'

Chapter 7

The clock on the bedside table read 5.15 a.m., but Alexa wasn't sleeping.

Curling her arm around Piet's waist, she ran her bare leg over his flank, coaxing him awake with kisses and caresses. He murmured in his sleep, gave a sigh of pleasure, then rolled over into her arms.

'A-Alexa?'

'I want you, Piet.'

He blinked, only half awake.

'But it's only . . .'

'I've been lying awake for hours, Piet, just fantasising about making love to you. And then I thought, why fantasise when you can have the real thing?'

Her fingers clawed lightly down Piet's chest and he growled, catching her hand and carrying it to his lips.

'What's come over you, Alexa? Suddenly you're insatiable.'

It was true. This last week, Alexa couldn't get enough of Piet. She felt sexed-up the whole time, hyper-sensitive to each and every stimulus. Even the argument she'd had with Damian had turned into verbal sex-play.

'Shut up and let me make love to you.' She stopped his protests with a kiss that began at his lips and travelled slowly and luxuriously all the way down to the base of his belly, stopping just short of engulfing his cock in glorious hot wetness.

Piet murmured and stroked his hand down her hair as she kissed all round the base of his cock: his inner thighs, his belly, the curling golden hairs that forested his balls.

'I always knew you were a sexy vixen,' he murmured. 'But these days you're so hot. Whatever has got into you . . . ?'

Alexa's heart thumped. An ocean of sensual warmth slooshed and tumbled in her belly, every nerve-ending crying out for more and still more pleasure.

'Remember what you said, about controlling things . . . ?'

'What about it?'

'. . . and people?'

'What *is* this?'

Alexa laughed softly. She was really beginning to get into this, riding high on the buzz of sensual power.

'You've really got it into your head that you control me, haven't you, Piet? But it's not true. Half the time you don't even know what I'm up to.' She ran her tongue up the underside of Piet's cock. 'Or who I'm doing it with.' Her teeth nibbled gently at the swelling flesh, now hardening to warm stone. 'Remember Aidan Kane?'

Piet tensed beneath her and rolled onto his side.

'Kane? You've heard from him again?'

This time Alexa laughed out loud.

'Jealous?' Excitement quivered through Alexa's body as

she sensed her new ascendancy over Piet. 'You should be. Don't you want to know what we did together?'

'As I matter of fact,' whispered Piet, his voice thick and heavy with expectation, 'I do.'

Alexa walked her fingers over Piet's smooth, golden flesh, feeling his muscles alternately tense and relax at her touch.

'Everything?'

'Every detail. Whatever you did to him, I want you to do it to me.'

He grunted with appreciation as Alexa licked delicately at the tip of his erect penis, lapping at its salty lubricating fluid as a kitten might lap cream.

'Remember that day I went to Swindon? To see a man called Protheroe?'

'You're telling me it wasn't Protheroe – it was Kane?'

The tongue lapped reflectively, the teeth nipping playfully at the desperately sensitive, wickedly delicious flesh. Making him wait just a little while longer.

'I had no idea until I got there. And when I found out it was one of his games, I almost turned round and came straight back . . . only I was curious.'

'And you wanted him?'

'Maybe. Maybe . . . just a little.' No, much more than a little, thought Alexa, recalling the powerful surge of wanting as Kane touched her for the first time, awakening countless dark, secret, guilty urges she'd kept buried for longer than she could remember. But as she lay beside Piet, teasing and caressing him, she realised that she wanted him every bit as much as she had wanted Aidan Kane.

'Where did you . . . ?'

'In a gallery. There were all these silent films playing, really dirty films of people wanking.' She took Piet's manhood in her hand and began stroking it lightly up and down. 'It turned me on.'

'You did it there – with him? In public?' She heard Piet catch his breath, and couldn't quite tell if he was excited or angry – or both.

'Behind a curtain. There were lots of people wandering about.'

'Did they see you?'

'I don't think so. I don't know.' She chuckled at the thought, it excited her. 'Yeah. Maybe they did. There I was, sucking him off and they were just the other side of that curtain . . .'

'God – no,' gasped Piet, his cock straining for release between Alexa's skilful fingers, his imagination working overtime. 'And . . . with *him*.'

'Then we fucked,' said Alexa casually, her fingers loosening their grip on Piet's dick so that they stimulated him to the point of frenzy, without any danger of bringing him to release. 'We did it standing up.'

'And?'

'I came. Twice.'

'Oh Alexa. Alexa, you hot bitch.' Piet seized Alexa and dragged her on top of him so that she was straddling his hips. She didn't put up much resistance. Her own storytelling had excited her just as much as it had Piet, and the white-hot rod of his prick sliced into her on a tide of slippery-wet desire. He arched his back, forcing himself very deep into her belly, letting her know that she was *his* hot bitch, not anybody else's and certainly not Aidan Kane's. 'You filthy, darling slut . . .'

'He was good,' she whispered tauntingly, through a mist of pleasure.

'Better than me?' demanded Piet with typical macho insecurity.

'He was . . . good,' she repeated, even now teasing him. 'Very good.'

Piet rolled round and flung her onto her back, straddling her from above, as if trying to re-establish once and for all who was in control of this fantasy. He fucked her hard, hungrily, like a man who has something to prove.

'Kane . . . I'll finish him, I'll crush him . . .'

'No,' whispered Alexa, returning Piet's frantic thrusts by raking her fingernails down his back. Oh but it felt obscenely good. 'No, we won't destroy Kane. We'll control him. Together. That'll be *much* more fun.'

But how, that was the question? Later, as they lay together in the darkness, rekindling desire in each other's bodies with teasing fingertips and tongues, they began to plot their sweet revenge on Aidan Kane.

'We need to know more about him,' said Piet.

'Know thine enemy,' murmured Alexa thoughtfully. And I don't really know him at all, she thought. Not the real Aidan Kane. Only the taste and scent of his body, and the shape of his cock between my lips. 'So how do we find out?'

'We find people who know him. We ask questions.'

'I suppose we could try the Arcadia Gallery, and the

bookshop. But they didn't seem to know him very well. They thought he was called Protheroe.'

'Bit of a mystery man, our Mr Kane. But no one can hide everything about himself. He has secrets, guilty secrets; perversions; filthy desires – and I want to know all about them.' Piet's teeth gently nipped the smooth curve of Alexa's shoulder. 'What about Boroughbridge Hall? Did you pick up anything on him there?'

'Only that he must have got access to my room somehow, otherwise how did he manage to film me with Suki Manderley?'

'Ah yes.' Piet's tongue circled Alexa's breast. 'The delicious Suki.'

'How do you know she was delicious?' retorted Alexa, faintly annoyed that Piet should be thinking about some other woman he'd never even met, when he was supposed to be making love to her.

'You make her sound that way; exotic. Adventurous. And besides . . .' Piet took Alexa's nipples between thumb and forefinger and pressed his thumbnails into the toughened flesh, provoking little ripples of sensual electricity.

'Besides what?'

'If we discount your peculiar fascination with Aidan Kane . . .'

'I am not fascinated with him!'

'Methinks the lady doth protest too much.' The pressure of the thumbnails increased perceptibly, turning the electric ripples into a regular, pulsing ache of unsatisfied lust. 'If we discount Kane, you have excellent taste in lovers. After all, you chose me.'

'Pig,' giggled Alexa, writhing in the grip of helpless pleasure.

'I should like to meet this Suki Manderley,' mused Piet, his voice dark and smooth as chocolate cream.

'Oh yes?' Alexa pouted in the darkness.

'I think we should begin our investigations with her.'

'Yes, well, you would. Any excuse.'

'Not jealous are you, Alexa? Oh, my little green-eyed vixen.'

'Don't talk rubbish,' said Alexa evasively. 'And isn't it you who ought to be jealous of me? I'm the one who had sex with her, remember?'

'Oh, I remember all right.' She could hear the excitement in Piet's voice. 'Such a pity I never got to see the pictures. Perhaps if I was to ask your Mr Kane *very* nicely . . .'

Alexa tried a different tack. She knew Piet; once he'd got an idea into his head there was no stopping him. Besides, there was a certain piquant excitement in the thought of rediscovering Suki Manderley. Together. Slithering her body over Piet's, she began rubbing herself all over him, massaging him with her nipples and the hard mound of her pubic bone.

'So where do we start?' she purred.

It was dark by the time Suki Manderley got home from work.

Parking her jeep outside her trendy barn conversion, she hurried up the path to the front door. It had been tougher going than usual at the agency, with wall-to-wall meetings which – even using the skills she'd learned at Boroughbridge Hall – Suki hadn't had much success in steering round to her way of thinking. The client wasn't happy with the pilot

TV ad, and when the client wasn't happy, the most junior account director invariably had to carry the can.

With a sigh of relief she slammed the door behind her and threw off her jacket. The ansaphone was flashing three messages but she'd leave it till later. Right now, what she needed was hot chocolate, a whole pint mug full of it, topped with whipped cream and spiked with a dash of cognac. Maybe one or two marshmallows to go with it, too. Then some pulp TV, before settling down to think up some revised ideas.

She clicked on the kitchen light, but never made it as far as the kettle. There was something propped up on the worktop, a bright red envelope stamped with a gold portcullis . . .

Horror chilled her blood, and she froze, shivering with shock. No! Not now, not when it had been so long that she had almost forgotten. With trembling fingers she picked up the envelope, tore it open, took out the rectangle of white card.

'PUT IT ON,' read the message. And there could be no doubt what it meant, for lying right next to the envelope was a black velvet scarf. A blindfold.

Suki's stomach turned over with panic. She darted glances around her. Aidan Kane. He must be here somewhere, watching her. How long had he been watching, how much more did he know about her that she'd never even suspected?

But there was more to this than fear or anger. Her fingers caressed the black velvet, thrilling to its softness, coaxed by its knowing sensuality. Put it on. Put it on.

She picked it up and pressed it to her face, closing her eyes to shut out the last glimpse of light a second before the velvet touched her skin. Swiftly she tied it behind her head.

'Tighter, Suki,' said a man's voice somewhere behind her. Shaking, she obeyed, tying the scarf so tightly that there was no possibility of cheating. 'What can you see?'

'Nothing. Nothing at all.'

'Good girl.'

Hands seized Suki from behind, wrenching her arms back so that she had no chance of resisting. She opened her mouth to cry out, but the next moment a damp, soft cloth was pressed against her face and she was filled with a sweet, sickly scent which turned her fear to a dizzy stupor.

And seconds later, everything went completely black.

In a comfortable but anonymous hotel bedroom, Piet took time to examine their captive.

Suki sprawled across the soft and expansive bed, stripped completely naked except for the blindfold, the velvet band closely moulded to her face. Her dark, silky hair fanned out on the white satin coverlet. Her lips were parted, and one hand raised to cover her breast as though, even in sleep, Suki wanted to hide from her own desires.

'She's even more delectable than I remember,' murmured Alexa, lifting Suki's sleeping hand and kissing the nipple beneath.

'Feline,' said Piet. 'Like a pedigree Siamese kitten.' He sat on the edge of the bed and teased the soft, dark mossy triangle between Suki's parted thighs. 'I wonder if she'll bite and scratch.'

'She's coming round,' said Alexa as Suki sighed and rolled onto her side, her fingers moving to the blindfold, exploring it. Remembering. Alexa was remembering too, recalling the night at Boroughbridge Hall when she had been the one wearing the blindfold. Her pussy ached with the memory of her guilty, uninhibited pleasure.

'Where . . . ?' gasped Suki sleepily.

Alexa slid onto the satin bedcover and, kneeling over Suki's face, hitched up her skirt. Underneath she was naked, and her own fragrance filled her nostrils as she lowered her freshly-shaven pussy onto the upraised lips.

'Drink,' she whispered, and had to bite her lip to stop herself crying out in exultation as she felt the long, muscular tongue wriggling around the softness of her most sensitive place.

Piet unbuttoned his shirt, hungrily but methodically. Kicking off his shoes, he unzipped his pants and stepped out of them. He was magnificently erect already, and Alexa wondered which of the two women filled his thoughts, which of them had coaxed him into throbbing hardness. Both, she told herself. This was Piet's greatest fantasy, made flesh.

'Hold still. Enjoy it.'

Pinning Suki's arms to the bed, she tightened her thighs about Suki's head and ground her pussy hard into the girl's face, relishing the power she now had over this unwitting rival. Her eyes did not leave Piet's face, making sure he got her silent message: I'm in charge, not your little mewling kitten. What turns you on isn't Suki's body; it's the sight of what I'm doing to it, and what I'm making her do to me.

Suki moaned into the wet folds of Alexa's sex, but Alexa wasn't about to let her go just yet. Sensory deprivation would make her all the more malleable. She began moving her hips back and forth, forcing Suki to fuck her with her tongue, enjoying the slight discomfort as nose and lips and teeth grazed over the hot, hard button of her clitoris.

Unbuttoning her chiffon blouse, Alexa let it float to the floor. She wasn't wearing a bra. It had excited her to drive all the way here, in the front seat of Piet's car, her breasts perfectly naked save for the flimsiest of diaphanous veils. Cold and excitement had turned her nipples into long, leathery stalks, and the nacreous globes of her breasts were marbled with delicate blue veins.

'Want me?' she mouthed silently at Piet, as she began circling her breasts with the flat of her hands, riding slowly and controlledly towards pleasure, keeping perfect silence even though her sex was beginning to pulse and throb, and the juices coursing out from between her labia were pouring down over Suki's face.

Piet's response was to climb onto the bed behind Alexa, sliding his strong arms round her waist and prising her hands from her breasts. His gruff voice whispered into the nape of her neck, delicious obscenities which took her to the very edge of orgasm.

'Darling slut. Beautiful, filthy-minded trollop. Cock-sucking angel . . .'

His hardness was drilling into the small of her back. Suddenly, violently, she wanted him. Suki's tongue was not enough to satisfy her, she wanted more. Letting herself sink forward, she lay on her belly on top of Suki, head to tail, and propped herself on her elbows with her buttocks in the air. Beneath her, Suki was shaking and gasping, her lips and chin covered with glassy wetness, her tongue licking greedily at the sticky sweetness.

'What's happening to me . . . ? Let me go . . .'

'That's not what you want,' chuckled Piet, enjoying the spectacle of Alexa's gorgeous backside, rising round and appetising above Suki's blindfolded face. 'I know what you want.'

Easing Alexa a few inches further forward, Piet straddled Suki's face. She squirmed a little as he slid his dick between her lips, but at the first taste of it she began to suck on it greedily, using the sharpness of her teeth just enough to give a satisfying sense of danger.

Alexa lay belly-down, her face between Suki's thighs, her back arched and her buttocks high in the air. Piet was kneeling behind her, she could feel his rhythmic thrusts as he mouth-fucked Suki Manderley, and for a few fleeting seconds, Alexa felt a pang of possessive lust. Well, if Piet could get his pleasure from Suki, so could she. Diving between Suki's outspread legs, she breathed in the exhilarating, vibrant scent of another woman's sex; the silky maidenhair freshly-washed and perfumed from the shower, yet not quite losing that unmistakable musky tang of arousal.

She plunged her tongue deep between Suki's labia, and was instantly intoxicated by the spicy sweetness which filled her mouth. Melting muscovado sugar, cinnamon, freshly-brewed arabica coffee, a thousand mouthwatering tastes met and mingled in this honeypot of never-ending nectar. And Alexa drank thirstily, so turned on by the taste of this helpless lover that she scarcely needed the extra stimulus of Piet's fingers and tongue, exploring and invading her backside.

'Aaah . . .'

In a moment of weakness she allowed herself to let out a single, almost inaudible sigh of delight. Piet's thumb was deep in her pussy now, his index finger on her clitoris, moving together, massaging her so lightly and so skilfully that he took her to the edge and held her there, maintaining the silky intensity of the pleasure without letting her take the last, blissful step into orgasm.

Suki tensed beneath Alexa's tongue. She felt her captive's body strain to lift itself off the bed, the pelvis tilting up, the mount of Venus forcing itself harder and harder against her mouth. Who was using whom? Alexa couldn't be sure any more. Was it Piet who was masturbating her to a climax, making spreading warmth turn to fire in her belly; or was it Suki, luring her to ecstasy by the sight and taste and smell of her pussy and nothing more?

Just when she thought there could be no more pleasure than this, Alexa felt Piet's tongue slide between her buttocks. She shuddered, writhed, resisted: momentarily ashamed of herself for wanting this so badly, this wonderful violation, this surrender of the last secret place. But her body rebelled against this last, ridiculous trace of prudishness. It was completely idiotic to plead outrage when she was licking the sweet, creamy oozings from the pussy of a blindfolded lover.

In the event, it was Suki who surrendered first, letting out a series of high-pitched gasps that were almost screams. The ooze between her thighs became a river, a waterfall, a raging torrent which overflowed Alexa's mouth; her sex-muscles fluttering around her tongue like the wings of some invisible butterfly.

It was all too much for Alexa. Pushing back against Piet,

she forced him to wank her harder and faster, seizing and devouring every last millimetre of pleasure his fingers and tongue could give her. Her climax was so dizzyingly intense that for a few seconds, she lost all sense of who and where she was, existing only in the tumbling waterfall of spurting, oozing joy.

Piet climaxed in a sudden loss of self-control which, ordinarily, would have annoyed him. Normally he liked to be completely in charge of his pleasure, not surprised by it. But how could he resent the exquisite rush of sensations which ambushed and overpowered him, flinging him into a deepening spiral of total satisfaction?

The three bodies lay in a jumbled heap for quite a long time, the white satin bedcover stained and disordered beneath them. Pleasure took many long moments to fade, and when Suki finally came to her senses, she found that her wrists were tied to the head of the bed. As Alexa untied the blindfold and slipped it off, Suki shook her head, blinking in the sudden light.

'You!'

Alexa laughed, darting a wavy line of kisses from Suki's pussy all the way up to her lips.

'That's right. It's been too long, Suki.'

And that was true, thought Alexa. The first time it had happened, even the second, she hadn't allowed herself to accept just how much fun it could be, getting it on with another woman.

Thick, strong fingers reached out to pinch Suki's still-hard, chocolate-button nipples. With an 'ouch' of discomfort, she screwed her head back. Piet was standing behind the bedhead, looming over her, an ironic smile on his lips.

'We haven't met,' he said. 'But Alexa has told me so much about you, I feel I know you already.'

'B-but I don't understand. The red envelope . . .'

'A trick,' explained Piet with simple frankness.

'I thought it was from . . .'

'Aidan Kane?' Alexa toyed with the silky tangle of Suki's pubic hair. It was wet with its own dew, and the excess had dripped down to form a dark, transparent stain on the bedcover. 'So you lied to me. You knew him all along . . .'

Suki nodded. There was real apprehension on her face.

'What do you want from me?'

'Just for you to answer a few questions,' soothed Alexa, already growing hungry for more of Suki's exotic pleasure. She could hardly decide which she preferred: to be Suki's mistress, or her slave.

'So.' Piet sat down on the edge of the bed and let his hand trail idly down to the moist triangle between Suki's thighs. 'You can start by telling us everything you know about Aidan Kane.'

Chapter 8

Suki Manderley gazed up imploringly at Piet and Alexa.

'Please untie me. The cords hurt my wrists.'

Her dark, almond-shaped eyes pleaded out of the delicate, high-cheekboned face. She looked so innocent and vulnerable, thought Alexa. Innocent with a hint of black widow spider. Alexa was beginning to wonder just who were the pawns in this game, and who the puppet-master. Or mistress . . .

'We'll untie you later,' said Alexa, sitting down on the bed next to Suki. 'When you've told us what we want to know.'

'But I don't know anything!' protested Suki, tugging ineffectually at the cords which bound her wrists to the bedhead.

'So you say,' purred Piet. 'But we don't quite believe you. After all, you lied to Alexa about knowing Aidan Kane. So we shall have to coax the truth out of you.' His eyes drifted sideways to Alexa. She knew what he meant by that look.

On the bedside table stood a shallow earthenware dish, heated by a candle underneath it, so that the oil it contained was warmed to just a little above blood heat. Taking a tiny bottle from her overnight case, Alexa added three drops of clear liquid to the oil. A rich, heavy scent wafted up from the warmed oil, filling the room with clouds of sweetness.

'A little something Piet picked up in the Dutch East Indies,' smiled Alexa, remembering the first time he had brought home the essential oil and introduced it into their lovemaking. 'Something to . . . relax you.'

She picked up the dish of oil and let it fall onto Suki's skin in a golden, viscous trickle; forming swirls and trails like golden syrup on her belly and breasts and thighs. It pooled in her navel, a deep well of golden fragrance, with tiny rivulets that escaped its banks and meandered slowly down over her flanks.

'Aaah,' gasped Suki, wriggling on the bed as the ordinary warmth of the oil gave way to something rather more subtle. A hint of spice, a burning sensation which was intensely pleasurable on the skin, but which might become a raging torment if the oil trickled between her thighs. 'What *is* this?'

Alexa moistened her hands with sweet almond oil and laid them on Suki's belly, spreading the massage oil with light movements.

'Tell us about Aidan Kane,' she whispered. And she stroked Suki a little harder, her fingers venturing upwards to the flattened globes of her breasts.

'I don't really *know* anything about him,' panted Suki, her lips moist with spittle and her brow misted with sweat. 'Truly I don't. Why are you doing this to me?'

'Are you and he . . . partners in crime?' demanded Piet,

sitting in an armchair beside the bed. 'Are you in this together?'

'In what? I don't understand.'

'Perhaps. Perhaps not.' Alexa was beginning to enjoy playing the femme fatale. She knew she ought to be ashamed of herself, but Suki made such a rewarding captive, and Alexa had never dreamed there could be such satisfaction to be had simply from having control over someone else's pleasure. 'But you do know him, you've already admitted that much.'

Her oiled hands circled Suki's breasts, the spicy elixir drawing her nipples into hard-tipped peaks. And all the time she kept up the pressure.

'You helped him set up the film he took of you and me together.'

'Film? No, no, I didn't.'

'You really expect us to believe that?' scoffed Piet.

'I . . .'

'You recognised the red envelope we planted in your kitchen,' pointed out Alexa.

Suki nodded.

'Yes. Yes, all right, I know him. Or at least, I did. It was a long time ago.'

'More,' said Piet. 'I want to know it all.'

Alexa's hands crept down Suki's flanks, lingering awhile on her hips, then the outside of her thighs.

'Open your legs for me, Suki.'

Suki's dark eyes narrowed. She pouted almost like a sulky child, determined to do the exact opposite of whatever she was asked to do.

'No.'

'Open them, or I shall have to make you.'

Alexa's voice was teasing rather than domineering. She wished Suki no harm. On the contrary, she was very fond of the girl, very sexually attracted to her too, though she wasn't at all sure that she should ever have trusted her.

Suki yielded with a disappointing lack of moral fibre, her smooth-skinned thighs sliding a few inches apart. Alexa felt the muscles relax under her fingers as she began massaging Suki's inner thighs, working her hands ever-closer to the small, hungry mouth of her sex.

'Now. Tell me about Aidan Kane. Where did you first meet him?'

Suki's eyes were closed, her head thrown back. She was breathing jerkily, fighting the treacherous warmth which Alexa knew must be spreading right through her body.

'It was . . . at a launch event for one of my advertising campaigns. For Venus Plus, you know, the Italian satellite sex channel . . .'

'And?' Piet leaned forward, his eyes not on Alexa's exploring hands, but on Suki's face; her tongue flicking constantly over her parted lips.

'It was my first big account, it meant a lot to me. Kane was there, at the press conference. Afterwards, he cornered me . . . told me he knew everything . . .'

Alexa and Piet exchanged glances. Alexa felt a shiver of recognition pass over her skin. She remembered only too well how Aidan Kane had told her he knew 'everything'; and he hadn't been bluffing.

'Everything about what?' she demanded.

'About how I won the account. You see, I . . . I got it by

agreeing to star in a porn movie for the owner's private collection. If the agency had found out . . . if it had been made public . . .'

So this was the hold that Aidan Kane had over Suki Manderley. Clearly he had perfected a tried and tested formula. Alexa wondered, with a kind of cold excitement, just how many other Alexas and Sukis there had been.

'What happened next?'

'He told me that once a month, when he summoned me, I must go to him and do whatever he wanted me to do.'

'And you did?'

Suki's dark eyes opened. A bead of perspiration trickled down her face.

'What else could I do? If I hadn't gone along with it . . .'

Her body almost lifted off the bed as Alexa's warm-oiled fingers slipped into the soft, deep well between Suki's thighs.

'No – please . . . aaah . . . no . . .'

Alexa ignored Suki's protests and poured a little more of the warm oil onto Suki's pubic mound, letting it drip down into the deep, moist groove of her pussy. She knew how it must feel, the tingling, the burning, the thousand tiny pinpricks of desire stabbing into her clitoris.

'How many times did you see him?'

'Five . . . no, six. The last time, he made me drive to Stevenage in the middle of the night.'

Piet's eyebrow shot up. This was perversion indeed.

'*Stevenage*? Good God.'

'It was pitch black and he fucked me on the bonnet of my own car. Then he left me there for the police to find, bound and gagged and covered in his come. That was the last I saw

137

of him, but ever since then I've kept looking over my shoulder
. . . until . . .'

She let out a little yelp as Alexa's finger and thumb lightly
pinched her clitoris.

'Until Boroughbridge Hall?' enquired Alexa.

Suki nodded glumly.

'He . . . he came to me. He told me if I helped him, if I
made love to you . . . it would be the last time, I'd never see
him again. I couldn't bear to be his slave any more.' The
almond eyes pleaded. 'Believe me, Alexa, it was no hardship
to go to bed with you. I fancied you like crazy the first time
I saw you.'

'Oh Suki,' breathed Alexa. 'Oh Suki, why didn't you warn
me about Aidan Kane?'

'I didn't dare.' Suki sobbed with pleasure as Alexa began
stroking her pussy, very delicately and tenderly, soothing the
burning flame of need and turning it to pure delight.

'More to the point,' cut in Piet, 'what else do you know
about Kane? What can you tell us, Suki?'

Suki turned her head sideways to look at Piet.

'Nothing. I don't know anything, please believe me.'

'But you must know *something*,' protested Alexa. 'After
six whole months.'

'Nothing,' repeated Suki. 'I don't know where he lives, I
don't know how he makes his money, I don't know how he
can make you hate him and want him at the same time.'

Nor do I, thought Alexa to herself. I only wish I did.

'And do you know the worst thing of all, Alexa?'

'What?'

'I don't even know who he really is. Who *is* Aidan Kane,

Alexa? If you ever find out, be sure and tell me.'

The next lunchtime, Piet and Alexa met up at a café in Montpellier. Alexa ordered café latte and vegetable terrine, even though she wasn't the least bit hungry, and then steered the conversation round to its inevitable destination.

'Kane,' she said. 'What are we going to do about Kane?'

Piet's stockinged foot toyed with her ankle under the table, his toes playfully climbing her leg.

'Good question. What do you think we ought to do?'

'Suki Manderley didn't get us very far, did she?' sighed Alexa, rolling the stem of her wine glass between her fingers. On the other side of the road, two young lovers were kissing in front of the window of an exclusive dress shop, practically devouring each other – much to the pretended disgust of passers-by. 'I really don't think she knows anything, she was telling the truth, I'm sure of it. She was just his pawn.'

'Then we'll have to follow a different lead, won't we?'

Alexa looked up, puzzled.

'A different lead? Piet, we haven't got *any* leads, Suki was by far our best shot.'

'That's where you're wrong, kitten.' Piet's toe insinuated itself between Alexa's knees, and wriggled into the warm haven beneath her skirt. 'Aidan Kane himself is our best lead.'

Alexa gave a hollow laugh.

'Oh yeah. Kane. And what do we know about him? Precisely nothing.'

'We know one thing, Alexa. We know that once every month, he's going to get in touch with you. He's going to demand that you keep up your side of the bargain.' Piet's golden eyes urged her to be one step ahead of him.

'Yes, but how does that help? All it means is that I'm some kind of sexual bond-slave to Aidan Kane, and we still end up no wiser than we were before. And,' she added, smiling briefly at the waiter who had brought her order, 'I for one have no desire to get fucked in Stevenage. Ever.'

'You won't have to, if my plan works.'

'Plan, what plan?'

'I was thinking. We could always bug him.'

Alexa almost dropped her fork into the puréed carrot.

'This *is* some kind of joke. Isn't it?' She wondered if she should burst out laughing now, or wait for the punchline.

'No joke, Alexa. I'm serious. I . . . er . . . do that sort of thing occasionally. I know people who know people.'

Alexa stared at him, utterly aghast.

'Piet,' she hissed. 'That "sort of thing" . . . it's illegal!'

Piet seemed perfectly unfazed by this possibility.

'In my line of work,' he shrugged, 'it pays to have just a little more information on your adversary than he has on you. And it strikes me that this might just work with Aidan Kane.'

Alexa took more than a little persuading, but Piet de Maas generally got his own way in the end. He could understand Alexa's reservations – she'd always been too honest for her own good, and he had given up trying to instil a little ruthlessness in her – but even though he'd never met Aidan Kane, he felt he was coming to know him intimately. His proclivities, his scams, his taste in wine and women, the way his mind worked. Above all, that he already knew the best way to get the better of him in the end.

The next day, he drove to the notorious end of Gloucester and parked outside Rhona's TV and Video Repairs. Such an ordinary-looking shop on the outside, tatty and old-fashioned even, with only a solitary satellite dish to suggest that the owner had kept up with modern technology. But Piet knew different. He knew Rhona McFee.

The doorbell jingled as he stepped into the shop. Rhona was trying to sell a second-hand TV set to a fussy man in a flat cap. Hardly a promising setting for such a glamorous woman, thought Piet. She flashed him one of her special smiles, pillarbox red lipstick outlining a mouth so large and fulsome that it could only have been designed by nature for oral sex.

'Hi,' Rhona greeted him in her soft Scottish brogue. 'I'll be with you in a moment.'

'It's OK. Take your time.'

Yeah, take as much time as you want, thought Piet. I'm enjoying just watching you. The way your body moves inside the tarty red dress which clashes so boldly with your naturally auburn hair; the way your legs reach right up underneath the short, short skirt and just keep on going for ever and ever. She was leaning over now, clinching the sale by flashing a good few inches of large, soft cleavage at the customer. He, in turn, was drawing a nervous finger round his scuffed red neck, easing the shirt collar away from his constricted throat. Piet knew just how he felt. Rhona McFee had that effect on him, too.

At last the customer left, with promises of same-day

delivery and a three-month warranty. The door rattled shut behind him.

'Did you give him what he wanted?' enquired Piet with lascivious good humour.

'Only the TV set,' grinned Rhona, turning the 'open' sign to 'closed'. 'Anything else is extra. So – what can I do for you this time, Piet?'

'Let's just say I want a little more than a beaten-up TV set. Shall we go into the back room and discuss it?'

Rhona was more than happy to comply. He followed a few steps behind, enjoying the sultry wiggle of her buttocks under all that red crêpe de chine; almost fixated by the seams at the back of her stockings. They were like road markings, leading the way if not to paradise, then at least to the kind of layby where you might pass a few agreeable hours.

The back room was the hub of Rhona's operations. As Piet had learned from a bent ex-Fraud Squad officer he happened to know, Rhona McFee was one of the top five experts in electronic surveillance in the entire country – not bad for a woman who supposedly ran an ailing TV repair business.

Rhona locked the door behind them, and perched on the edge of a workbench littered with microphones, bits of wire, unravelled microcassettes and a disembowelled alarm clock. Hands resting on the bench behind her, she threw out her truly magnificent chest. Piet could have wept to see the way it jiggled, completely unrestrained, beneath her dress.

'Well? I take it this isn't a social call. Who's been getting up your nose this time?' She winked. 'Or is your woman giving you the runaround?'

'That's not important. But I do need your expertise.'

'Ah well, you know I always give complete satisfaction. But do *you* have what *I* need, Piet?' A long, varnished fingernail the colour of arterial blood teased down his cheek and pushed its way playfully between his lips.

'If you mean, can I pay . . .' Piet reached into his inside pocket for the large wad of new fifty-pound notes he had brought with him.

Rhona laughed.

'Oh, I take it for granted you've got the money. You've got more money than my mongrel dog's got fleas. But money's not everything, Piet; sometimes there are other things that people need.'

'What's that supposed to mean?'

Piet felt a cold finger of invisible desire stroking the sleeping serpent of his dick. Rhona McFee was a dirty-minded slut, a backstreet seductress whose voice alone was enough to make a grown man spurt. Rhona slid off the workbench with a whisper of cheap satin and a glimpse of red French knickers.

'Get to the point, Piet. What is it you want?'

'There's someone I'm . . . investigating. I need to know where he is and what he's up to.'

'I might be able to help.'

'And I want to be absolutely sure he doesn't suspect he's being bugged. This needs to be very, very discreet.'

'Ah. Well, that will cost more. A lot more.'

'But you do have something?'

Rhona looked at him as if he was mad.

'Of course.'

She took a small key from her pocket and unlocked one of the metal cabinets ranged around the walls. Taking out a PVC wallet, she tipped a tiny metal button into her palm.

'The Celeste DX2 personal tracker. Pretty, isn't it?'

'May I?' Piet took it from Rhona's hand and turned it over. It really was tiny, smaller than a watch battery. 'What can it do?'

'It'll give you audio transmission over thirty miles, and locator transmission over eighty.'

Piet whistled his approval.

'OK, so I'm impressed. How much?'

'What are you offering?'

'Say, the usual, plus ten per cent.'

'Make that twenty. Plus . . .'

'What?'

'This.'

Rhona wrapped herself around Piet like spider-silk, her body soft as a duck-down duvet underneath her red dress. Her lips fastened on his, her fingers expertly unfastening his tie and letting it fall to the floor. There was no mistaking what the gesture meant; her belly was already grinding against his dick, and since he was a normal man with normal desires, the proposition seemed a perfectly reasonable one to Piet de Maas. Rhona McFee was anything but unappealing. Screwing her wouldn't be much of a hardship.

'You know, Piet, I've always had this . . . thing for you.'

'Is that right?'

'You should be flattered. Normally I charge a thousand quid a night.'

Piet laid the DX2 very carefully on the worktop, then

took off his new Lauren jacket and slung it over the back of a chair. You had to get your priorities right.

'You're a dirty-minded streetwalker, Rhona McFee.'

'And what does that make you?'

Rhona's fingers fluttered down, undoing the buttons on his shirt. He was perfectly happy to let her think she was seducing him. Why not let her do all the work, if that was what turned her on? Piet was relishing the feel of her hot, soft body against his dick, the tickle of her long, sharp nails as they uncovered bare flesh.

'Quite a nice one,' commented Rhona, sliding his prick out from its hiding-place, examining it like an expert on the *Antiques Roadshow.*

'Thanks,' replied Piet with a half-smile. 'I'm honoured you like it.'

'The question is, do you know what to do with it?' Rhona hiked up her skirt and wriggled her red French knickers down over her bottom, leaving her standing before him in black suspenders and seamed stockings. What a shameless hussy she was. Piet found himself liking her better with every second that passed.

He didn't bother answering her question in words; just took her by the hips and sat her on the worktop, facing him.

'Mind the merchandise,' snapped Rhona as bits of metal slid and rolled in all directions. But her protest faded to a stifled giggle as Piet pushed her legs wide apart to display the ripe, fruity folds of her sex.

'Don't worry. I know exactly what I'm doing,' replied Piet, pulling open Rhona's button-through dress to get at the quivering pink flesh beneath. He nuzzled into the vast

softness of her bosom, his lips and teeth encircling rubber-
hard nipple flesh as his dick drove deep inside her.

Piet knew there were other ways of doing business, sure
there were. More conventional ways, more ethical too. But
few of them quite as enjoyable as this.

As Alexa pointed out, the main sticking-point of Piet's plan
was that you couldn't bug a person if you didn't know where
they were. Which meant that Alexa would just have to wait
until the next time Aidan chose to get in touch with her.

If he chose to. Alexa reminded herself of what had
happened to Suki: six monthly orgies that had ended as
abruptly as they began, and then nothing more – not a word
from him until he had turned up at Boroughbridge Hall. She
wondered if she would last the full six months, and if Kane
had already lined up the next in his repertoire of sexual
conquests. Funnily enough, although the thought made her
angry it made her feel something else much more strongly:
regret. Little by little, she was becoming hooked on a
dangerous sensual obsession.

She was changing, too. Ordinary fantasies no longer
satisfied her the way they used to. At work, she found herself
picturing sex scenes with the people she worked with, even
the ones she didn't remotely fancy. Sex was becoming her
work, her hobby, her passion. Every moment she was alone
with Piet, they were either screwing or thinking about
screwing. And over everything loomed the invisible, silent
spectre of Aidan Kane.

It was Piet who suggested practising with the bug. If Alexa
was going to plant it successfully on Kane, she needed a

trial run. Which was how Alexa came to be listening in on a conversation taking place in Damian's office. A dangerous occupation, maybe, but exciting too. At lunchtime, she sat in her own small office and listened in through the headset Piet had got from Rhona McFee.

There were two people involved: Damian and Sonia. And their conversation was definitely not about shorthand dictation. First came Sonia's breathless squeak:

'You're a very bad baby.'

'Bad enough for a spanking?'

'The baddest baby in the whole wide world.'

Then a series of ringing slaps, delivered with such force that Alexa could hardly doubt Sonia's enthusiasm. Perhaps she was getting her own back on Damian for all the times he'd played headmaster to her naughty schoolgirl.

'Bad, bad baby.'

Alexa had to put her hand across her mouth to stop herself laughing. The idea of Damian baring his fat little buttocks for his secretary to spank was so visually comic that she couldn't get it out of her mind, even when she'd taken off the headphones and put them into her desk drawer. Any more of that, and she'd never be able to look Damian in the face again. She wondered if Aidan Kane would turn out to have ludicrous secrets, too. Secrets? Yeah, surely. But ludicrous? Somehow she doubted it.

She tapped into her e-mail address and opened up her mailbox.

'ONE NEW MESSAGE.'

Good. That would be the stuff she'd asked for from the sub-office in Sacramento. She called it up.

What she found on her screen came as something of a surprise. This was certainly not background information on a new chain of Japanese noodle bars. It was a kind of cartoon; a five-second animated sequence showing a bizarre tangle of naked bodies, all ages, both sexes, in every sexual permutation you could possibly imagine. Cocks in mouths, cocks up arses, tongues in pussies, multiple cocks spurting into and over naked flesh, wide open thighs and big, soft breasts. The more you looked, the more you saw, the more obscene it all appeared. And the more exciting.

Alexa gaped at the screen, her breath coming in fits and starts. But she wasn't looking at the pictures any more. Her gaze was fixed on the message which had just appeared at the bottom of the screen. She didn't need to guess who that message was from. It consisted of a numbered sequence which Alexa quickly realised must be a map reference, and one other thing. A single word.

'NOW.'

Chapter 9

There wasn't time for Alexa to contact Piet, even if she'd thought of it – and she hadn't. Her mind was far too full of Aidan Kane to think about anything or anyone else, her chaotic thoughts surfing a turmoil of anger, fear and delirious expectation.

No time to get changed, either. No time to do anything but concoct a feeble excuse to barge in on Damian, so that she could sneakily slip the bug into her handbag, and then clear off with some vague story about having to go to the printer's to check some last-minute proofs.

It wasn't until she was sitting in her car in the staff car park that Alexa took a moment to pull herself together. For fuck's sake, she didn't even know where she was going. There was an OS map in the glove compartment and she took it out, unfolding it and searching for the co-ordinates she had jotted down on a scrap of paper.

What? She wrinkled her nose in disbelief. But if she'd got this right – and she was pretty sure she had – Aidan Kane was proposing to meet her somewhere at the top of the steep escarpment overlooking the east side of Cheltenham. In other words, slap bang in the middle of nowhere.

She glanced down at her feet. Black patent ankle-boots with three-inch heels were hardly the recommended footwear for clambering all over the Cotswolds on a damp March day. There were Wellingtons in the boot, but she was buggered if she was turning up to a clandestine rendezvous wearing gumboots.

'Damn you, Kane,' she hissed between clenched teeth as she headed out towards Cheltenham. Why am I doing this? she wondered as she drove along, occasionally casting a glance at the overcast sky. You whistle and I come running. Piet has a plan and I go along with it.

Don't deceive yourself, Alexa, said a small voice in her head. You planned it too. You've been half-crazy with excitement this last month, just waiting for Kane to call you. You only pretend to be angry because it makes you look less like a cheap slut.

And it was uncomfortably true. How many times, when she was in bed with Piet, had Alexa closed her eyes and imagined that Aidan Kane was standing in the corner of the bedroom, arms folded, watching with those hooded eyes and that dark, ironic smile? She could imagine him right now, sitting in the passenger seat as she drove, his hand on her thigh, pushing her skirt and releasing the scent of her guilty desire.

Half an hour later, Alexa reached the far side of Charlton Kings, and parked in the hotel car park which had been conveniently placed at the foot of the escarpment. A fine drizzle was misting down out of the greyish air, and she pulled up the collar of her jacket as she squinted up the slope. It was steep, green, a mixture of irregularly shaped fields and scraps of ancient woodland, clinging determinedly to the rocky hillside. There were cows in those fields. And sheep. Maybe she ought to wear the Wellingtons after all.

Dismissing that pathetic thought from her mind, she set off up the winding track, passing a man in an anorak and walking boots, on his way back down. He nodded a greeting.

'Not going far like that, are you? You'll catch your death.'

'I'll be fine.'

'Well watch it near the top, the mud's as slippery as ice.'

How typical of Kane to humiliate her like this, thought Alexa, trudging up the hillside. The road gave way first to a gravelly footpath, then to a barely-discernable track leading diagonally across a cow-pasture. It was raining properly now, pissing a constant stream of water down the back of her neck; and naturally her inadequate boots were letting in water and other, less pleasant things as she squidged her way across the sodden grass.

To one side lay a shallow, scooping slope leading down to a stone-built farmhouse. Smoke curled up out of the chimney, and for a moment Alexa imagined herself sitting in the kitchen, warming her wet feet on the Aga and drinking pint mugs of tea. She forced herself to turn away and trudge on, sometimes having to use hands as well as feet to grab tufts of foliage and stop herself sliding all the way back down.

Before her, black and shadowy woodland was strung out along the skyline. According to the map, Kane would be waiting for her somewhere beyond that dark line of trees. Mind you, with his sense of humour she would probably arrive to discover a life-size cardboard cut-out and a one-word message: Sucker. With more than a few misgivings, she climbed on into the twilit world of the forest.

'Ouch. Bloody hell.'

She rubbed her twisted ankle and tried not to look down as she climbed makeshift wooden steps which had somehow been hammered into the mud and rock. To her right the ground fell away almost vertically; the only thing holding the hillside together seemed to be the tangle of scrubby trees and shrubs. To her left, and above, there was nothing but forest, steeply climbing and twisting towards a distant patch of grey sky.

Twigs snapped underfoot. A rabbit darted out from cover and disappeared into a patch of blackthorn. Something scuffled about in the undergrowth near her right foot, and she prayed that she'd be out of this godforsaken place before dark set in.

Pausing for breath, she called out.

'Kane? Are you there?'

Her own voice answered her, but there was no other sound save the flutter of wings as a startled wood pigeon launched itself above the canopy of trees.

'Kane, don't you *dare* fuck me about.'

If she'd hoped to draw him out, she was disappointed. Nothing moved, no shadow turned into the tall, rangy shape of Aidan Kane. She would just have to keep on walking.

It took another ten minutes to reach the brow of the hill, emerging out of the trees into a misty grey light which made her blink after the darkness of the forest. The whole of Cheltenham was spread out before her, like a toy village set among soggy papier mâché hills. But it wasn't the view that brought Alexa up short.

Aidan Kane was standing exactly where he'd said he'd be, perched at the very top of the scarp, gazing down; damp but immaculate in his dark suit, and not in the least bit muddy. He spoke first, not bothering to turn round.

'You took your time.'

'What!' Fury roared like a furnace inside Alexa as rainwater coursed down her face, sticking her hair to her forehead, reaching cold, wet fingers down her back and soaking her clothes.

'I said, you took your time.' This time Kane did turn round. In profile he looked more than ever like an eagle, sharp-featured and imperious, and as he turned to face Alexa his grey-green eyes turned to dark shadows in his high-cheekboned face. 'Oh dear.' The corners of his mouth twitched as though he were suppressing a smile.

'What the hell is *that* supposed to mean?' Alexa flicked wet hair out of her eyes.

'Only that you don't look as if you've had a very easy time of it.'

'Oh really? And whose fault is that?' Alexa squared up to him, eyeball to eyeball, still panting from the climb. But Kane wasn't about to be unsettled. His eyes travelled down from the matted, tousled mane to her sodden jacket, ripped stockings and ruined ankle-boots.

'You could have worn proper shoes, those are less than useless.'

This was too much for Alexa. In a furious reflex, she slapped his face. Hard. He didn't even flinch. On the contrary, he seemed to quite like it.

'Oh my little hellcat. How very passionate you are.'

She wriggled out of his grasp as he made to plant a kiss on her cold and shivering cheek.

'Don't you dare touch me. Leave me alone.'

'That's what you want, is it?'

'I said—'

'I know what you said, Alexa. But forgive me if I'm not entirely convinced.'

This time Aidan really did smile, a fact which only served to madden Alexa. What was it about him? How did he manage to do this to her every time? He had only to look at her and she loathed and despised him, and wanted and yearned for his caress.

'You can think what you like,' she said sullenly, forcing herself to break eye-contact and staring down at the ground. Her heart was thumping in her chest, her damp and shivering breasts were covered in gooseflesh and rubbing uncomfortably against the lacy cups of her bra.

'Have you any idea how fetching you look like that, all bedraggled, with your wet skirt clinging to your thighs? Your nipples are hard as iron underneath that jacket.'

She stared at him.

'How . . . ?' Silly question. She bit her lip.

'I've told you before, Alexa,' Kane said gently, taking Alexa's chin between his fingers and planting a long, moist, proprietorial kiss on her parted lips. 'I know everything. Or at least, everything that matters.'

Alexa's fingers slid into the pocket of her jacket. It was still there, the little metal button. All she had to do was find a way . . .

'Why have you brought me here?' she demanded, drawing slightly away.

'It's a great view, don't you think?'

'Kane . . .'

'Don't you get an incredible power-buzz, just looking down on everything and everybody?'

'You mean, the way you look down on me?'

Kane laughed. This time, when he pulled her towards him, Alexa didn't struggle. She used his kisses as an opportunity to slip the DX2 into his jacket pocket.

'Look down on you? I regard you as a challenge.'

His hands smoothed back the wet hair which the wind had whipped against her face. They were hot, dry, powerful, and she felt the throb of his heat entering her body, exciting her, breaking down her better judgement and reminding her that whatever else he might be, Aidan Kane was also the most exciting lover she had had in a very long time. Perhaps ever.

'Come here,' he said, taking her by the wrist and pulling her closer to the edge of the escarpment. She hung back, she'd never liked heights and she was mentally reliving that horrible moment at Gloucester Docks, balancing a hundred feet above bare concrete and dirty estuary water.

'W-why?'

'I want to show you something.'

He drew her towards him and she found herself balanced right on the edge, next to him.

'Show me what?'

'This.'

She ought to have known it was a trick, but it wasn't

until he dragged them both over the rim of the escarpment that she realised and tried to pull back; by which point, of course, it was far too late.

Alexa let out a scream of terror as they dived into nothingness. Her hands clawed and grasped at Aidan, and their bodies clung together as they rolled over and over, hurtling down the hillside, branches and brambles scratching and biting their flesh.

I'm going to die, thought Alexa as the world spun in her head, sky turning to earth, then branches, then sky and earth again. But she was wrong again. Seconds later – though it seemed more like hours – they came to a halt, their tangled and torn bodies fetching up against the base of a gnarled hawthorn.

Alexa opened her eyes. They were no more than twenty yards down the slope, and the town still lay far beneath them. Her blouse had ripped and her skirt was up round her bottom, revealing the semi-transparency of wet white silk knickers. Kane was lying half beside her, half on top of her, his hand on her breast; and Alexa was ashamed to realise that she was shaking, not with fear but with exhilaration.

'Bastard,' she snapped. 'You could have killed us.'

'Anything, Alexa,' replied Kane, lifting up Alexa's bra to expose her cold, goose-pimpled breasts. 'We can do *anything*. Anything we want.'

She moaned as his teeth met in her flesh, and his tongue flicked warm and wet across the ice-cone of her nipple.

'Aidan . . .'

'Life is nothing without danger. And there's no one here to see us or hear us, whatever we desire we can have. The only limit is our own imagination. Don't you see?'

The wind whipped at Alexa's bare flesh like the tongues of lascivious devils, punishing and exciting. And in that instant she *did* see. Her fingers clawed at Aidan's shirt, ripping it open. His chest wasn't like Piet's, golden with a forest of curls; it was smooth and hard, lean with muscle and bone. She pressed her lips to the dry, warm skin and teased it with her teeth. There would be no going back. Not now.

It was a bitterly cold March afternoon, grey with freezing rain, but Alexa didn't notice the cold any more. She was far too busy undressing Aidan Kane. Mud caked her skin as Kane stripped the blouse and skirt from her, unfastening her bra and dropping it onto the wet grass, where it was immediately rolled into the mire. Her numb fingers fumbled with Kane's trouser-zip, then pushed his trousers and pants down over his hips, unpeeling his secret fruit.

Semi-naked in the mud, her hair in wet rat's tails and rainwater dripping from her nipples, Alexa climbed astride Kane's slim-hipped torso. His dick slipped smoothly into her and he took her by the hips, setting the rhythm of her bareback ride.

She reached back and took his balls in her right hand, scratching and caressing as she pumped her thighs, squeezing her pussy tight about his shaft. It wasn't easy, keeping a foothold on the steep, slippery slope. The two muddy bodies slipped and rolled about in the mud, pebbles and wet grass violating every secret place like sharp teeth and wet, probing tongues. Flesh slithered across flesh, smearing soil and sweat and sodden leaves in weird patterns.

The world was spinning. Bodies were rolling and tumbling, clawing and biting. This wasn't civilised lovemaking, nor a fumbled screw behind a curtain in a private movie theatre. It was animal lust, expressed with a complete lack of inhibitions; the fast track to absolute sexual satisfaction. Like Kane had said, there was no one here to see or hear or disapprove. They could do anything, no matter how depraved, no matter how shockingly perverse. Alexa felt Kane's fingers probing her anus; one, two, three, pushing deep into her, stretching her beyond the point she had believed possible. He was opening her up, turning her inside out, exposing the complete hypocrisy of her resistance.

Alexa had lost track of where her flesh ended and Kane's began. The only thing she knew for certain now was that excitement was pulsing through her body, pumping every nerve-ending full of the electricity of desire.

It felt like the ultimate liberation. And when Alexa came, it was with a great wolf-howl of release.

'You planted the DX2?'

'Of course I did.' Alexa felt faintly annoyed that Piet could doubt her. Hadn't they planned and practised this for weeks? 'I slipped it through the lining of his pocket, he'll never find it.'

'And it's working?'

'Come and see for yourself. But hurry, Piet. We don't have long.'

'I'm on my way.'

Alexa put down her mobile phone and settled down to wait for Piet to arrive. He'd need to drive like a maniac, the audio signal from the bug had already faded almost to nothing and they couldn't risk Kane getting out of range of the locator transmitter. If need be, Alexa would have to take up the chase on her own.

She shifted on her seat, wondering what Piet would make of her when he saw her, still caked with mud and stinking of sex. Kane's seductive smell was strong between her thighs, her pussy bare, wet and tingling beneath her muddied skirt. She smiled, without meaning to. She would answer all Piet's questions, but perhaps not in full detail. There were some memories you wanted to keep to yourself, for your sole and private enjoyment.

On the small, round screen a moving dot of yellow light flashed regularly against a dark green background, showing the direction of the signal. It seemed to be coming directly from the southwest, constant and strong. All they had to do was follow it, and they would start to get answers to all the questions they had about Kane.

The funny thing was, Alexa was beginning to feel distinctly uneasy. It wasn't that she was afraid of confrontation, but she couldn't help wondering if she'd live to regret solving the mystery that was Aidan Kane.

She had to wait almost an hour before Piet's grey Merc came bumping through the twilight, jiggling inelegantly over the rutted track and into the car park. He jumped out and wrenched open the passenger door of Alexa's jeep.

'Alexa, I—'

Their eyes met. Piet's opened wide at the sight of Alexa, scratched and bruised and bloodied, mud smeared all over her face, rainwater dripping down onto her torn and ruined suit from rat's tails of sodden, dishevelled hair.

'Good God, Alexa, what ever happened to you?'

She could hardly resist the obvious reply.

'Aidan Kane happened to me. Now get in quickly and shut up. If we don't hurry we'll lose him.'

Piet's jaw fell open. He wasn't used to having Alexa talk to him this way. He kind of liked it.

'Shouldn't we take the Merc?'

'No, we need the jeep, we don't know where the hell he's leading us. Could be halfway up a bloody mountain by now.' She surprised herself with her own brusqueness, reaching across Piet and slamming shut the passenger door. 'Here, take the monitor, you'll have to navigate.'

Piet took it without a murmur, taken aback by Alexa's sudden – and rather fetching – dominance.

'It's fading, go left. Faster, I'm losing the signal . . .'

With one eye on the road and the other on her mud-spattered reflection, Alexa drove westwards into the remnants of the sunset, as recklessly as she dared.

'It's taking us onto the motorway,' muttered Piet. 'Look, do you want to swap seats and I'll drive?'

Alexa silenced him with a look that said, 'Don't you think you've done enough already?' and picked up speed to join the motorway.

'It's getting stronger,' announced Piet.

'Good.'

They cruised along at seventy, Alexa resisting the urge to go faster since she was bound to ruin everything by getting stopped for speeding. The signal was good and strong now, a regular blip-blip-blip on the screen, and some of the tension began to ebb out of her body, slackening the aching muscles in her shoulders, letting her breathe more easily.

But there was another kind of tension remaining, another kind of warm, deep ache that she didn't want to lose. And that was the ache of remembered satisfaction, still making her body glow all over. Even now, she could feel the sharpness of Kane's teeth, the smooth warm silkiness of his tongue, the hot hardness of his manhood, plunging between her thighs again and again and again.

'Alexa.'

She snapped out of her trance and looked at Piet.

'Mmm?'

'Alexa, are you sure you're all right?' Piet's hand caressed her thigh, muddied and bare beneath her torn stockings.

'I'm fine.' She shivered, reliving the dizzying moment when she and Kane had tumbled down that slope, clawing and scratching at each other like starving wildcats, desperate to slake their sexual hunger.

'But Alexa, you're bleeding.' Piet traced the line of a half-dried scratch which wound its way up her leg, disappearing under the tattered hem of her skirt.

'And you only just noticed? Look Piet, I'm fine, really I am. Don't fuss.'

'Tell me what happened.' Piet's eyes were almost pleading with her. 'Please, Alexa. I want to know.'

Alexa savoured the power of knowing something that Piet desperately wanted to know. It was quite a turn-on. Perhaps she was beginning to understand why Aidan Kane got such a buzz from knowing other people's secrets. Then she relented.

'I will. But not now, later.'

They drove on, the darkness thickening around them. It soon became obvious where they were going.

'He's heading into Bristol,' said Alexa, almost disappointed – though she couldn't think what else she'd expected. A midnight rendezvous at Stonehenge? Orgies at Glastonbury Tor?

'Shh, listen – we're getting the audio signal back. What *is* that noise?'

Alexa shook her head, baffled.

'Water? Running water?'

'Could be down by the river.' Piet stared down at the screen. 'Take a right here . . . now a left. It's really strong now. He's slowing down.'

Alexa's stomach turned a backflip. It was happening, just the way they'd planned it. She'd planted the bug on Kane and now he was leading them to him, not suspecting a thing. It was all too easy, and now she wasn't even sure that she wanted to know the secrets he'd been hiding. Once the secrets were gone, would the desire follow?

The audio signal continued to be as baffling as ever, nothing but the indistinct swish and gurgle of water, then a kind of hissing like sausages in a pan.

'He's here somewhere,' muttered Piet as the jeep headed towards the covered market, rattling over cobblestones as Alexa took a sharp right into a narrow alleyway. A drunk mouthed some kind of unintelligible curse and lurched out of the way as they drew up alongside the locked door to the market. 'But where . . . ?'

'There.' Alexa opened the door and jumped down. She

pointed into the distance, towards four or five people huddled around a doorway.

'How can you be sure?'

'I can't. But it's the only sign of life around here.' She started walking purposefully towards it, ignoring the open-mouthed stare of the drunk as his eyes fixed on her bare thighs and filthy, ripped clothes. 'Looks like some kind of night club.'

Piet fell in step beside her, slipping the monitor into his pocket.

'Well, it's a dive,' he commented. 'Exactly the sort of hole where you'd expect to find a worm like Aidan Kane.'

Alexa wasn't listening. She was walking up to the doorway, weighing up the situation. It was unusual all right. Two gay gorillas with muscles and chains, doormen she guessed from the joke bow-ties. A tall blonde woman in fun-fur hotpants and black thigh-boots, completely naked from the waist up, unless you counted the nipple-rings and the dog-leash to which they were attached. A PVC-clad dwarf on the other end of the leash, his masked face leading down to a thick neck encased in a studded collar, a powerful torso criss-crossed with shiny straps and a naked cock, stretched to surreal length by a little silver weight swinging from its pierced tip. And just behind him, an elderly man dressed like Shirley Temple, complete with ankle-socks and shoulder-length blonde wig.

As Alexa took a step forward, Piet put his hand on her shoulder.

'You're not thinking of going in there . . . ?'

'What else do you suggest? Unless you've lost interest in Aidan Kane.'

That was enough to push Piet forward. One of the gay gorillas looked him up and down.

'Membership card?'

'I don't have one.'

'Then you can't come in.'

'I'll join.'

'Sorry, membership's by personal recommendation only.' The lipsticked mouth pouted in a camp, candy-pink kiss. 'And you're not really my type.'

'Oh, I don't know,' cut in his even more muscular friend, giving Piet's biceps a really good squeeze. 'I could force myself.'

'What about me, then?' demanded Alexa, squeezing between Piet and the Shirley Temple clone. Critical eyes looked her up and down. Eyebrows shot up. Heads nodded.

'Mmm, unusual. Like the torn underwear.'

'You'll do, sweetheart, in you go.' A broad wink. 'And don't do anything I wouldn't.'

'Sorry Piet,' said Alexa. 'Looks like I'm on my own on this one.'

Piet's expression darkened to thunder as Alexa swept by.

'Now hold on—'

'No, you hold on, darling. Mmm, you *are* a big boy, aren't you?' Strong hands grabbed Piet and held him fast, while others explored his body, not sparing any modesty. He swore and kicked out as fingers closed around his dick. 'Feel the size of him under those chinos, and that lovely tight backside. Oh, how sweet, he's getting a hard-on. Fancy giving me one do you, big butch boy?'

Alexa escaped down the stairs and into the basement club. Part her felt a little scared. She'd been to a few dodgy clubs in her time, sure she had, in the years before she met Piet. But that had just been playing at being sexually weird. Those clubs had all been full of self-conscious, middle-class people desperate to develop hang-ups: the sort who thought all you needed to become a sexual deviant were leather pants, a nose-stud and a close friend to lick your bottom.

But this was different. This really was . . . unusual.

'Welcome to Heaven,' said a naked man whose head was encased in a shiny, black, studded sphere that made it look like a sea-mine.

'Heaven?'

He handed her a flower from the silver quiver slung around his shoulders. She sniffed it and her head began to spin.

'The only place where all your dreams come true. Here, you can come and be anything you want to be.'

'Anything?'

'Anything at all, no questions asked, all expectations set aside. Here, an archbishop can be a housewife and a housewife can be a whore. Enjoy.'

He was gone. Alexa felt very strange, her senses confused yet sharpened by whatever had been on that flower. Without thinking, she raised it to her face again, ran its soft petals over her cheek, breathed in its fresh, light scent. Wow. The colours in here. They were really incredible . . . And the smells, they seemed to fill her head. Sweat, a dozen different brands of perfume, massage oil, pussy-juice, semen, piss, plastic and body-warmed leather . . .

Weird. And too erotic for words.

'Love the gear,' breathed a girl as she danced past, her lovely body quite naked under filmy veils of loosely-wrapped white chiffon.

'Th-thank you.' It wasn't until the girl was gone that Alexa began to wonder if she'd been a girl at all. She had breasts, sure; gorgeous plump breasts that defied gravity and bounced invitingly on her chest as she danced. Lovely long blonde hair too. But could you be a girl and still have a twelve-inch penis, soaring in a hard, smooth arc out of a thicket of ash-blonde curls? It was all so very, very confusing.

She made her way slowly across the dance-floor to the bar, fighting to clear her head. Music played softly beneath the undercurrent of laughter and talk. People talked or danced or kissed in the shadows, huddled into twos or threes or mysterious, swaying groups. The air smelt intoxicating, every breath plunging Alexa deeper into a sweet, seductive trance.

There were two people standing by the bar, not that they were there to drink. They were in full Edwardian dress, a man's dark suit with cravat and white gloves, a lady's evening gown of buttermilk-yellow muslin and matching ankle-boots with tall, tapering heels. They were kissing and caressing, running their hands over each other, totally lost in their shared fantasy. Only one strange thing made Alexa stop and stare: the man was a woman, and the woman was a man.

'What can I get you?' asked the barman, his face zipped into a white leather mask which matched his immaculate tuxedo.

'Nothing . . . maybe just a—'

'A glass of mineral water?' suggested the barman, taking a glass from underneath the counter and sliding it across the bar-top. 'I hope sparkling is OK.'

Alexa stared at it. There was something sitting at the bottom of the glass, something small and round and silvery, covered with an accumulation of bursting bubbles.

At that moment Piet arrived, red-faced and agitated.

'Alexa! Thank God you're OK. You *are* OK, aren't you?'

Alexa pointed to the glass of water, and the silvery disc which had floated right to the bottom.

'Look,' she said. Piet's gaze followed her pointing finger, and he let out a groan, slamming his fist down on the counter. For once, Alexa knew exactly how he felt.

For sitting at the bottom of Alexa's glass of water was the Celeste DX2.

After the incident at the Heaven Club, it was days before Alexa could persuade Piet to leave her alone in the house. Though they didn't speak about it, they both knew what he was afraid of. The all-seeing, all-knowing spectre of Aidan Kane. Alexa was afraid of it too, but in a rather different way.

She *wanted* to be afraid.

At last she was on her own. She celebrated by taking a long, deep, hot bath, wallowing in scented bubbles until she was drowsy, relaxed and hungry for pleasure. The warm water circulated lazily around her body in miniature whirlpools and eddies, the tiny currents shimmering between her thighs, sliding into the well between the lips of her sex.

The bar of soap seemed to creep down her belly of its own volition, leading her hand down over the smooth, taut skin to the thicket of red-brown curls and the plump hillock which guarded the entrance to her sex. Slowly the soap slid over her mount of Venus, the pubic bone hard and sharp underneath the cushion of soft flesh. Another inch, another millimetre, and it would plunge down the waterfall of her sex, into the moist and sensitive valley between her outer labia. It would be easy to masturbate, with long, sweeping strokes, using the stinging lather to stimulate the swollen head of her clitoris, skating over her own wetness until pleasure blossomed into ecstasy.

But what would she dream about as she was pleasuring herself? Would she be reliving one of her old fantasies, lying on a tropical beach underneath some over-endowed Hollywood hunk? Or would it be Piet de Maas's tongue slipping between her thighs as the bar of soap teased her to the perfection of pleasure? Or someone else . . . ?

Alexa smiled to herself and placed the bar of soap back in the dish. The water was getting a bit cold anyway. Pulling the plug, she got out and wrapped herself in the biggest, warmest, fluffiest white towel imaginable. Outside it was a dismal March day, a grey earth under a grey and drizzly sky, cold and dank. But in here it was warm, steamy, sensual and fragrant. The central heating was on high, the bedroom was tropically welcoming and the crisp clean bedspread was smooth and soft and inviting.

Going across to the wardrobe, Alexa opened it and slid open the drawer where she kept her most intimate possessions, her 'toy box' as Piet called it. This was where she kept the things she used to give herself pleasure, with or without Piet.

There it was, her very favourite sex-toy; the very largest of her collection of vibrators, fashioned out of smooth, semi-translucent black rubber which almost exactly mimicked the warmth and texture of living flesh. Ah yes. Twelve inches of perfect, solitary pleasure, fragrant with use and begging to give her pleasure once again.

Stretched out on the bed, Alexa switched on the vibrator and ran its buzzing tip over her face, letting it slide over her cheeks, her nose, her eyelids, her lips. It was a lover's dick, urgent and strong, and she put out her tongue and licked it. The taste of her own juices filled her mouth, reminding her of just how good it felt to come.

The rubber tip quivered and throbbed over her throat and down to the foothills of her breasts, climbing a circular path to the summit. She turned up the vibrator to maximum. Could she bear the brutal, grinding sensation on her nipples? She cried out softly and writhed on the bed as she tormented herself, squeezing her breasts together with one hand and holding the vibrator against her nipples for as long as she could bear.

A cool dampness was spreading across the bedspread between her thighs, as juice welled out of her sex, trickling in honeysweet droplets into the deep furrow between her buttocks. She wanted it, oh, how she wanted it.

Her black rubber lover was hungry for her. With a two-handed thrust she pushed him inside her, her hips bucking to meet the thrust and swallow him whole. It felt good; she was in control, she could have anything she wanted. Anything. Harder – and all she had to do was thrust the vibrator into her with a little more force. Faster, stronger, the vibrator buzzed to a crazy crescendo, pumping in and out of her sex. Wetness trickled and oozed and dribbled over her fingers, inundating everything. She'd have to change the bedspread again, or Piet would notice.

Not that it was Piet she was thinking about. She didn't need a man, not any man, that was what she kept telling herself when the shadowy figure floated back into a corner of her consciousness. Not you, Kane, not anyone, understand? This is my pleasure and you don't have to give it to me – because I'm taking it, hot and strong and just the way I like it.

She could feel the need to climax building up inside her, like the pressure of lava building up inside a volcano. Not much further, and she would reach the point of no return. Here it was, coming, coming, coming: a furnace-heat that began as a gradual warmth in her belly and spread out in vast, rippling waves that finally consumed her whole body and soul in a kind of starburst of white heat.

At the very moment of orgasm, Alexa surrendered to the raw impulse within her and screamed out loud:

'You're there, aren't you? I know you're there. Don't you want me?'

The question hung in the air for what seemed an eternity. Then pleasure exploded inside Alexa and the fragments came whirling down like dust in the sunlight.

As Alexa sprawled, exhausted, across the bed, a tall, lean figure appeared in the doorway. A moment later Aidan Kane walked into the bedroom, as cool as anything. He looked down at Alexa and smiled.

'As a matter of fact I do.'

Chapter 10

Alexa made no move to cover herself. She stared up into Aidan Kane's face, the black vibrator still wet and buzzing between her paralysed fingers.

'You *knew*. All the time, you knew.'

Kane sat down on the edge of the bed, took the vibrator from her and switched it off. The silence closed in around them, forming an invisible cage of lust.

'Of course I knew.' He sounded almost exasperated. 'An entertaining display, why don't you do it again?'

He amused himself by trailing the dripping tip of the vibrator across Alexa's lips, down over her chin and into the deep valley between her breasts. As it skimmed the taut flesh of her belly she seized his hand and held it fast.

'How did you find out?'

'About the bugging device? That hardly matters.'

'Not to you, maybe!'

'And besides, why should I reveal the tricks of my trade to you? In any case it was a very rudimentary device,' he added. 'You can scarcely have imagined it would deceive me for long. But I confess I was impressed by your . . . initiative.'

'You?' Alexa managed to say. 'Impressed by me? This *is* a red letter day.'

Her shoulders were heaving, her breasts quivering as she dragged long, juddering breaths into her body. It was no use pretending to be outraged, whenever she was with Aidan Kane everything else lost out to raging, uncontrollable lust.

'Sarcasm doesn't suit you, Alexa.'

Kane knelt over her on the bed, casting a dark, batlike shadow over her. She pushed against his hands but he was much stronger, his sheer body-weight pinning her down by her shoulders. And why put all your energies into fighting something you'd been secretly longing for? Bite me Lord Dracula, whispered a silly, secret voice in her head. Pierce my flesh and take me and make me yours . . .

'Kane . . .'

He stopped her feeble protests with an all-consuming kiss that engulfed her mouth, catching her breath in her throat and filling her with the sour, curiously seductive taste of stale wine.

'Now, white lace and nothing underneath – that suits you,' he said softly, releasing her from the cage of his kiss. 'Mud on bare flesh, semen trickling over red satin knickers, or how about thigh-high boots and a PVC corset, laced so tight you can hardly breathe? I know what suits you, Alexa. And I know what makes you tick.' He wound a strand of her hair about his finger and tugged it tight, making her gasp. 'So why did you do it? Why did you plant that bug on me?'

'If you know everything about me you can work that out for yourself.' She squirmed underneath him, not so much trying to escape as trying everything in her power to force

Kane to make hard, fast, dominant love to her.

'Perhaps I prefer to hear it from you. From these beautiful lips.' He trailed the end of the lock of hair across Alexa's mouth, watching it flinch at the touch, the rose-pink flesh puckering and pouting in spite of itself. 'It's strange, but I can imagine them wet with blood. You'd make a captivating vampire, Alexa.'

He licked his lips, and her eyes followed the flick of his tongue-tip, thirstily imagining it lapping nectar from her pussy, or smearing cool saliva over tiny, fire-hot bites in her all-too-willing flesh. Dracula in Armani, the Dark Count in handmade shirts.

'So you're determined not to tell me, Alexa? But it's all so very obvious.'

Kane's knees nudged Alexa's thighs wider apart, releasing the full power of her musky scent, far stronger and sweeter than the rose-scented oil she had bathed in. And then he put his lips together and began to blow currents of cold air between her legs, never once touching her sex but using his own breath to stimulate and torment her. She closed her eyes and moaned softly, but Kane would not let her close her thighs and escape her punishment.

'Obvious,' he repeated, and directed a slender draught of breath between the petals of Alexa's pouting labia, causing her clitoris to quiver on its long, fleshy stalk and filling her with shivers of hot and cold and base desire. 'Any fool can see how strong the need is in you.'

She fought her own weakness, and forced herself to confront him, the way she had promised herself that she would.

'You said you wanted me. So take me. Fuck me.'

'Oh Alexa, how you tempt me.'

Her heart leapt, the warmth of her sex turning to a throbbing heat as he unzipped his pants and took out his penis. She'd somehow forgotten just how beautiful it was, what incredible power it held over her. And now he was going to give it to her, end her agony of longing, push inside her and make her come until at last exhaustion took the place of desire. She knew in that moment, to her shame, that she would do anything, *anything*, just to have that dick inside her and be fucked so far beyond the point of pleasure that the word no longer held any meaning.

'You want it?'

'You know I do.'

'What do you want?'

'I want you to . . .' Her eyes gleamed, her tongue flicked hungrily across her lips. 'I want you to fuck me.'

'Poor Alexa,' sighed Aidan. 'Such a slave to your desires. And I thought I was beginning to teach you the rudiments of self-control.'

He took his cock in his hand. Oh, it was such an incredible thing, that rod of stiffened flesh, slightly curving, marble-smooth and hot and pink and juicy purple at its tip. Alexa thirsted for the taste of that fat purple plum on her tongue, to squeeze out its juice and let it trickle in salty streamlets down her throat.

But Kane was still playing games with her. He held himself just out of her reach, stroking and pumping his manhood tantalisingly close to her lips. She put out her tongue and tried to lick his balls, swinging low over her mouth, but though she tried again and again they were always just out of reach.

That was her punishment for wanting to know more than she was allowed to know; and it was such a beautiful punishment, one that brought her far more pleasure than pain. She watched, mesmerised, as Kane's dick jerked once, twice, again, again, again; then she felt the hot spurt of his seed, falling like gluey raindrops on her upturned face, covering her eyelids, her cheeks, her lips, her throat, with splashes of sticky opalescence.

He didn't need to tell her what to do. She put out her tongue and licked the last, pearly oozings from the tip of Kane's dick, desperate with hunger and thirst for him, silently pleading with him to understand how much she needed to be fucked, here and now.

'Still hungry, Alexa?'

'Please . . . now . . .'

Her lips strained to close about his dick, to swallow it down, to take it prisoner, but he drew away.

'No. Not now, you'll have to wait.'

'Aidan, you bastard . . . you can't do this to me! Not again!'

She almost wept as he pushed his still-hard dick back inside his trousers and zipped them up.

'Patience is a virtue, Alexa,' was his parting shot as he walked out of the bedroom door.

'I didn't bother washing,' purred Alexa as Piet stepped into the kitchen and sniffed the air. She was sitting at the kitchen table, still loosely wrapped in the fluffy towel and sipping coffee. 'I thought you might like me better this way.'

'What the hell . . . ?'

Piet's voice tailed off, the colour draining from his face. He took in the evidence of his own eyes: Alexa's matted hair, the white flakiness on her cheek and throat, the wetness on the breasts that peeped over the top of that once-white bath towel, the secret sparkle in her dark eyes. Not to mention the unmistakable, alley-cat perfume which had hit him the minute he walked into the room. He swallowed hard.

'He's been here, hasn't he?'

'Who?' enquired Alexa, innocently, teasingly; unsatisfied lust scripting this seduction scene to perfection. She adjusted her towel, showing just the right amount of cleavage, making sure that Piet would very shortly be well-hooked and wriggling on her line.

'Aidan Kane, who else?'

'What if he has?'

Anger flared on Piet's face as he jumped to the worst possible conclusion.

'You waited for me to leave just so you could get together with Kane. You've been planning this all along, haven't you?' He sounded just like a petulant schoolboy.

Alexa laughed softly, getting to her feet and sliding her hands round Piet's waist.

'Calm down darling, it wasn't like that at all. I was having a bath . . . he just turned up out of the blue.' She kissed Piet on the neck, making sure he got the full benefit of her very special fragrance. 'I guess he must have been watching the house.'

'And?' Piet put a whole world of meaning into that one small word.

'And . . . nothing.'

Piet fingered the still-sticky tress of matted hair which hung down Alexa's right cheek.

'It doesn't smell like nothing,' he growled. 'You stink of sex.'

'We didn't do anything,' Alexa assured him, easing off his tie and beginning to unbutton his shirt. 'Or at least, we didn't have sex, if that's what you mean. Kane just came here to gloat. He . . . tied me down and then wanked over my face.'

'He *what*?'

'I guess it was his way of telling me I'd been a naughty girl.'

'I'll kill him,' seethed Piet. His expression was so thunderous that Alexa burst out laughing.

'But Piet – this was all your idea in the first place! You're the one who wanted me to go along with this, to screw Kane so you could find out more about him. You're the one who thought of bugging him . . .'

'Ah. But you *like* screwing him, don't you?' Piet's eyes searched Alexa's face for any sign of treachery. 'Admit it – it's got so you'd rather have him in your bed than me!'

'Don't talk rubbish.' Alexa kissed Piet's chest, letting her kisses follow the line of the buttons as she unfastened them, one by one. 'It takes a *real* man to give me what I need.' She let her gaze travel upwards until she was looking into Piet's blue eyes. 'Think you've got what it takes to satisfy me, Piet? I've got one hell of an appetite. Remember that fantasy you had, about screwing me over the kitchen table?'

The next thing she knew, she was sprawled face-down over the worktop, strawberry jam in her hair and spilt coffee soaking into her towel. Not that the towel stayed wrapped round her for long, for in one swift and impatient movement Piet had whisked it off and dropped it on the floor.

'Ready for afternoon tea, Alexa? Let's start with peaches and cream.'

She giggled excitedly as she heard the fridge door open, then close; then felt a sudden, delicious coldness attack her bare skin. In a trice she realised that Piet must have grabbed the pot of clotted cream from the fridge and emptied it all over her backside. She could feel it trickling slowly down her lower back and into the cleft between her buttocks; over the swell of her arse-cheeks and drip, drip, dripping with soft plopping sounds onto the tiles.

'Still hungry for me, Alexa?' hissed Piet.

'Oh. Oh yes,' she groaned, as Piet's fingers scooped and smeared the cold, thick cream over her skin, insinuating it between the peachy cheeks of her bottom. Her cheek was squashed down uncomfortably hard against the wet formica, but she was impervious to anything but pleasure now. 'Oh darling . . .'

Alexa's groans and mews rose to a high-pitched crescendo of excitement as Piet's dick scythed deep inside her, not entering her pussy but using the cream to lubricate the tight sphincter of her anus. Oh, but it felt good, squelchy and sticky and forbidden. It felt better still to know that somewhere, somehow, Aidan Kane might be watching, getting more unbearably jealous by the moment.

And that soon, very soon, he might just do something about it.

In the back room at Rhona's TV and Video Repairs, Piet set about getting answers to some of his questions.

Rhona McFee looked particularly alluring today, in that endearingly tartish way she'd made her very own. An ensemble consisting of four-inch red stilettos, black-seamed stockings, a clingy black minidress with a deep scoop neckline and dangly red earrings that clashed cheerfully with her plum-coloured lipstick and fiery auburn hair was enough to turn any man's mind from the task in hand. But Piet was here on business, he had no intention of being distracted . . . or at least, not until he'd got what he came for.

'So what's the problem?' demanded Rhona, perching on the workbench with one foot balanced on a chair, revealing one stocking-top and a black lacy suspender.

'That Celeste DX2 you let me have. It let me down.'

'Really?' Rhona looked surprised. 'Normally they're very reliable. Of course, they're still in the experimental stage, so you do get the occasional operational difficulty. How long into the transmission did it break down?'

'It's hard to say,' replied Piet drily.

'Was it a problem with the audio signal? We do sometimes get interference from mobile phones . . .'

Piet coughed uncomfortably.

'It's neither,' he confessed.

Rhona folded her arms.

'What then? I'm not a mind reader.'

'Actually, it was found.'

Rhona's neatly-pencilled eyebrows shot up to her hairline.

'Found? You're kidding.'

'I wish I was.'

'But with something so small, you could only find it if you knew what you were looking for.' Rhona looked intrigued now. She slid off the worktop, and her skirt wriggled down over her thigh. 'Who were you following, James Bond?'

'A tall, dark guy, I don't suppose you'd have heard of him. Grey-green eyes, mean-looking mouth. Goes by the name of Aidan Kane, but for all I know it's an alias.'

Piet was so busy being hypnotised by Rhona's huge and mobile breasts, gently rising and falling beneath her dress, that he completely missed the look of worried recognition which briefly crossed Rhona's face. A second or so later, it was gone.

Rhona took the bug from Piet's hand.

'Good God, what happened to it? It's all rusty.'

'It got . . . er . . . wet.'

'Well, never mind about that now.' Rhona dropped it into a drawer. 'I'll sort it out later.' Her long, surprisingly slender fingers curled about Piet's tie and pulled him towards her. 'I suppose you'll be wanting your money back?'

'Well, I can think of other kinds of compensation.'

'I was hoping you might say that.'

He braced himself against the door as Rhona slid down his body. There was someone ringing the shop bell, but neither of them took the slightest bit of notice. Piet looked down at Rhona, her eyes fixed on his and her lips curved into a knowing smile as she pulled down the stretchy scoop neckline of her dress and her wonderful breasts popped out over the top.

Oh, but they were immense. White, fluffy, gloriously expansive as cumulus clouds. And now Rhona was unzipping his aching dick and wrapping her breasts around it, imprisoning it in the nicest way he could imagine.

'You're a wicked woman, Rhona McFee. Depraved.'

'Shut up and enjoy it, before I change my mind.'

Well, Piet wasn't one to look a gift horse in the mouth. And it was hard not to enjoy being given a tit-wank by a woman like Rhona. How big were those breasts? Thirty-six double-D? E? F? Much more than could ever fit into your cupped hands, or your mouth, that was for sure. He growled with pleasure as the smooth, white flesh slid back and forth along his shaft, moulded tightly to his dick by her skilful hands. And when she put out her tongue and started licking his glans each time it emerged, missile-like, from between the clouds . . .

It was all too much to take.

He did, at least, manage to remain silent as he came, splashing abundantly all over Rhona's breasts. To have shouted out at the moment of climax would have been profoundly undignified. His mouth filled with the taste of salt where he had bitten his lip, but frankly he couldn't have cared less about the pain.

'Call it a consolation prize,' smiled Rhona, playfully licking the cream from her own nipple.

Piet grinned.

'I'd rather call it the first instalment.'

* * *

Days passed and turned into weeks. Alexa waited patiently, no longer hoping but knowing that Aidan would come to her. She was certain now that he was as addicted to this game of cat and mouse as she was.

She'd always enjoyed her work, but it seemed dull now; the excitement of winning the big account was as nothing compared to the intoxication of having Aidan Kane's pleasure in the palm of her hand.

Mmm. She daydreamed at her desk, daydreamed at home, daydreamed even when she was sitting in the multiplex with Piet. One of the games they'd always enjoyed playing was to take seats right at the back of the theatre and explore each other's bodies as everyone else was watching the film.

The slight spice of danger had always turned them on, wondering if that fat brunette might stop cramming popcorn into her mouth, turn and catch a glimpse of a hand disappearing between bare, widespread thighs. Or whether the man in the hat might overhear a stifled giggle and, turning to complain, stare open-mouthed at the woman fondling her lover's cock through his pants.

An innocent enough game, fun too. But even Piet's expert fondling in the warm, flickering darkness couldn't compare with daydreams of Aidan Kane. Alexa fantasised about how it would happen, when the next summons would come. What form would it take? Would she be sitting in the middle of a business presentation when he walked in, snapped his fingers and spoke that one, deliriously sexy word, 'Now'?

Or might she be asleep, one night when Piet was away on business? She shivered as she imagined the tall, dark figure silhouetted against the bedroom window; the curtains fluttering, translucent in the moonlight; the voice, smooth and imperious. 'Now.'

She ached for that moment, masturbated to the rhythm of her fantasies, closed her eyes and imagined a thousand different ways in which Aidan might call her back to slavery. Piet was getting impatient with her, irritated by her excitement; she knew he was starting to have cold feet about the whole Kane affair, but as she told him, that was just too bad. He'd started it and she was going to finish it. Whatever it might take.

One Wednesday lunchtime towards the end of April, she went shopping in Cirencester. Perhaps it was her overheated subconscious which drew her towards Whispers, the lingerie shop near the marketplace. She stood for quite a long time outside the window, asking herself which of the exotic creations would be most to Aidan's taste. Perhaps the black strappy nightgown, slashed to the thigh and plunging to the waist? Pure Pussy Galore. Or the pretty white basque, sprinkled with tiny pink satin rosebuds? Very Jane Austen, very chaste and vulnerable. There were so many possibilities, so many ways to turn a man on.

She pushed open the door and stepped inside, intending to buy nothing more than a new bra or a couple of pairs of knickers. But the atmosphere was so seductive that she couldn't help lingering over the trailing suspenders, the slinky straps, the softly padded bra-cups.

'Can I help you?' Tina, the middle-aged proprietor, got up from her chair. She was looking in Alexa's direction, yet Alexa had the strangest feeling that she was looking through rather than at her. She seemed . . . dazed. Drugged even. Not like Tina at all.

'Are you all right, Tina? You don't look well.'

'I'm fine.' The muddled gaze seemed to fight to resolve itself. 'Can I show you something?'

'Just some plain white lace briefs . . .'

Completely ignoring the rack of briefs, Tina went across to an old-fashioned wooden display cabinet and slid open one of the glass-fronted drawers.

'This is nice.'

Alexa stared at the weird garment Tina was holding out to her. Weird? No, weird was too flattering a word for it. It was just plain tasteless. And what exactly was it? A sort of teddy, she supposed, though really it was scarcely more than a criss-cross of semi-see-through scarlet nylon, the open crotch blatantly edged with horribly scratchy fur fabric, mimicking pubic curls.

'Tina, it's horrible!'

She waved it away, but Tina was inexplicably determined.

'It's nice, Alexa, you should try it. Really you should.' The eyes almost pleaded.

'Just the knickers, please, Tina. I can't imagine why you'd think I'd be interested in a horrible thing like that. It's . . . it's so . . . tarty!'

Tina took Alexa's hand, prised open the fingers and wrapped them round the teddy.

'I really think you should try it, Alexa. It's you, it really is. Like it was *meant* for you.'

It was only then that Alexa realised. Kane. This was all his doing. Hurriedly she stepped into the changing cubicle and drew the curtain. She turned the teddy inside out. Yes! Pinned inside was a message, one of Aidan's summonses. A brief list of directions, followed by a four-word command: 'Wear this for me.'

She dangled the fur-trimmed nylon from between her finger and thumb. Yuk. Did Kane really expect her to wear *this*? The disappointment inside her was almost too much to bear. All this fantasising, and now he was becoming duller than she'd ever imagined possible.

Just as well she was about to become wilder than he could ever dream.

Chapter 11

As soon as she got back to the office, Alexa phoned Piet.

'Yeah?'

'Piet, it's Alexa. It's happened.'

There was a silence on the other end of the line, as Piet drew in breath. Alexa sensed he'd been hoping that the last incident would be the ultimate, the finish. Little did he know . . .

'Kane? He's called you?'

'I have the time and the place, it's tonight. You'll have to bike some of my things over to me here, there's no time for me to come home first. They're in a suitcase on top of the wardrobe . . .'

'Now just hold on, Alexa! Do you know what you're saying?'

Alexa leant back in her chair, eased off her shoe and wiggled her toes. She was beginning to enjoy herself.

'Of course I do. I'm saying that tonight, I'm going to meet Aidan Kane, and we're going to . . .'

'Alexa! I don't want to hear this.'

'Really? I thought you wanted to know all the details.'

'Yeah, well, maybe I've changed my mind. Look, Alexa,

you don't have to go, Kane has nothing on you.'

Alexa laughed softly.

'You've got it all wrong, Piet. I don't *have* to, I *want* to.'

Piet groaned. She could feel his frustration vibrating down the telephone line, but more than that, she could feel his excitement. He was breathing hard, like a man who was more turned-on than angry.

'You're all hard for me, aren't you Piet?'

When he replied, it was in a tortured hiss of breath.

'Damn you.'

'Poor Piet. You hate yourself for it, don't you? But you shouldn't. It's only natural to be excited by the idea of your lover having wild sex with a disreputable stranger. I wonder what Kane is planning to do to me this time.'

'Alexa. Shut up, Alexa . . .'

'Hush, listen. You know you want to.' Alexa closed her eyes and let her imagination run riot. 'I bet he has a special place all prepared for me. A dungeon. I can see it now, whips and chains everywhere, and he strips me naked and ties me up . . .'

Alexa couldn't be sure what this was doing to Piet, but it sure as hell was turning her on. She could almost feel Kane's hands on her, brutally wrenching her arms behind her back, forcing her to her knees, making her do unspeakable things to him . . .

'He's put manacles round my wrists, they're so heavy. And oh, it's cold in here, cold and damp. I can hear water running down the walls and dripping onto the floor. I'm shivering.'

'Oh God. Alexa, stop this.'

'He's chaining me to the wall, stretching out my wrists and ankles so I'm pinned and hanging there like a starfish. My face is to the wall, I can't see anything. My legs are wide apart and I have no more secrets from him. He can even see into the cleft between my buttocks. Oh, he's touching me there, tickling me with something, a feather I think . . . Oh Piet, I can't stand it! My anus is contracting, winking, now it's opening up and inviting him in . . .'

She paused, listening to Piet's breathing on the other end of the line; hoarse, heavy, almost an asthmatic gasp. He was close to coming and so was she.

'He's taking a whip to me, Piet, he's hitting me across my buttocks. It stings! It feels like sharp teeth, biting into my skin. It burns like hell, but now the feeling is changing . . . it's softer, warmer, it makes my whole body ache. I know what I want and he knows too. He's grabbing my buttocks and pulling them apart, opening me up, thrusting into me, making me come even though it hurts and I hate him . . .'

'Aaah. Alexaaaa . . .'

She listened to him climax, the stifled gasp followed by a long, shuddering sigh, then silence.

'Feeling better now, Piet? Be a good boy and send my things over.'

Replacing the receiver on the hook, she looked up. Damian was standing in the doorway, staring at her like she'd just beamed in from another planet. She wondered how much of her conversation he'd heard. Not that it mattered. It was about time Damian began to see her in a whole new light.

Alexa drove towards Oxford, taking her time, deliberately

not hurrying even though her body was tense with excitement.

She stole an admiring glance at her reflection in the rearview mirror. It was surprising how realistic fake furs could be, she mused. The sable coat felt cool and heavy and just a little tickly on her naked flesh, and she wasn't used to the spike-heeled, patent leather boots, which rose thigh-high to kiss the swollen petals of her sex. Oh, but it felt good.

Beside her, on the passenger seat, lay the box containing the vile red nylon thing (she refused to think of it as a garment), together with Aidan's note. Even now, she could hardly believe that he had wanted her to wear something so revolting. No, not revolting. Ordinary. The kind of thing a middle-aged housewife would buy at an underwear party, in a vain attempt to seduce her coarse, loutish husband. Just plain ordinary. Well, well, Kane, she thought. I never had you marked down as a closet suburbanite.

Turning off the A40, she headed for the centre of Oxford. At least he'd had the good taste to pick somewhere with a little class. Mind you, the address he'd given her would probably turn out to be some broken-down shack, or a council maisonette on the Blackbird Leys estate. That was the kind of sense of humour Kane had.

But no. Alexa smiled with approval as she drove towards number 99, Balliol Approach. This was no shack. This was the Maisley Court, Oxford's oldest and most select hotel.

The doorman flattered her with a double-take as he held open her car door for her. She dangled the keys over his palm like a chocolate drop over a dog's mouth.

'If you could just park it for me.'

'Certainly madam, right away.'

Well, her calf-length coat might not be real sable, but it certainly made Alexa feel like a countess. She swept up the steps and into the foyer of the hotel, taller than usual by a good five inches on account of her spiky heels. If only she had a beautiful black panther, snapping and snarling on the end of a golden leash. That would provide the essential finishing touch to this perfect ensemble.

As she rested her gloved hand on the desk, the boy on reception turned five shades of crimson and adjusted his collar. His voice came out as a strangled squeak.

'Can I . . . ?'

'Help me? Oh I do hope so.' Alexa allowed her gloved fingers to caress his small, childish hand and he leapt back as though she'd just given him an electric shock. 'The Imperial Suite.' She smiled. 'I'm expected.'

'Ah . . . yes. That's on the second floor, just opposite the lift. Shall I ring the gentleman for you?'

She coaxed his hand away from the telephone receiver.

'No. Don't bother. I'd like this to be a surprise.'

She stepped into the lift and the doors swished softly shut behind her. In a moment she would step out onto the second floor, knock on the door of the Imperial Suite, make her grand entrance.

Her mouth was dry, not with the beginnings of fear but with the adrenaline rush of pure exhilaration. She had planned this, not Aidan Kane. And it was going to go exactly the way she'd planned it. Her way.

The lift stopped with a jolt, and she stepped out into piped muzak and pale pink walls. Inside the small cardboard box which dangled by its ribbon from her fingers, a scrap of scarlet nylon slid about with a muffled scuffling noise. Her boots made a soft thudding sound on the deep-pile carpet as she crossed the corridor to the door with the brass plate that read 'Imperial Suite'.

As she raised her hand to knock, she realised that it wasn't locked; it was ajar. With a deep breath she pushed it open and walked straight in.

'Hello Aidan. Pleased to see me?'

For once she had caught him off-guard, lying on the bed staring up at the Europorn channel on the overhead TV. He leapt up and stared, a smile creeping over his lips.

'You could say that.'

He took his time, letting his eyes drink in the full effect. She felt them travelling upwards from the polished toes of her boots to the all-enveloping sable coat, wickedly sensual, each exquisitely simulated hair glistening in the soft electric light. Black leather gloves, a diamanté necklace and matching earrings, hair teased and piled into a froth of curls and tendrils. Black kohl eyeliner and smudged grey shadow; rouge-noir lipstick that accentuated the pout of her large and hungry mouth.

'Venus in Furs. Nice, Alexa. Very nice.'

Nicer than you think, Alexa told herself. *So much nicer you just won't believe it.*

'Glad you like it,' she said non-committally, making no attempt to get any closer to him. Kane walked towards her, his eyes straying to the triangle of bare flesh just visible above the neckline of the sable coat. She had to make a special effort not to smile with triumph.

'You got my gift?' Kane asked coolly.

'Your *gift*?' This time she sneered at him, her glossy lips curling with disdain. 'Oh – you mean this?'

Her fingers tore at the thin cardboard, reducing the box to shreds, and threw the resulting mess onto the floor, grinding the red nylon teddy under the heel of her boot.

'That's what I think of your cheap little gift, Kane. I thought of burning it, but you'll probably want to get your money back.'

Kane's flecked green eyes sparkled with interest. Alexa knew she was exciting him, knew he'd never seen her like this, angry yet in complete control. And it seemed to her that they had both grown weary of Alexa the victim. Now it was time for Alexa the mistress.

'You didn't like it.' He smiled. 'What a pity.'

'You insulted me,' she spat back. 'Made me look cheap.'

'Oh really? I thought that was what you liked, Alexa. To play the cheap little whore . . .'

For an instant, she imagined her gloved hand striking him, slapping his smug face, taking the revenge she'd craved for so long. But no. That wasn't the way she'd planned it. She wouldn't give him the satisfaction of thinking he'd provoked her. Not this time.

'This is my idea of a gift, Kane,' she said, her voice scarcely louder than a whisper. 'I think you'll approve.'

Slowly, lingeringly, she released the hooks which fastened the sable coat. For a few seconds she held it shut, letting Kane imagine what might be underneath, knowing that whatever he could dream up would be nothing like as good as what was really there. Then she released the coat, and let it slither down over her shoulders, forming a soft drift of rippling black about her feet. A tamed and sleeping panther, curled about her booted ankles.

She kicked the coat away. Her eyes defied Kane to be anything less than overwhelmed.

'Well?'

She saw him shudder, and his eyes widened as he took in the full magnificence of her almost-naked body. The diamanté necklace sparkled brilliantly above the twin peaks of her breasts, their pink crests emerging from between a criss-cross of PVC straps, which crossed in a black X between her breasts then joined to a belt which cinched her waist. This led to other straps and chains, which disappeared between her legs, isolating and throwing into relief the completely shaven mound of her sex, pink-white and soft above the thigh-skimming tops of her tall, shiny boots.

'Oh Alexa,' breathed Aidan. And for the first time ever, she saw him lost for words.

'And I have another present for you too. Aren't you impressed by my generosity?'

Alexa was thoroughly enjoying tormenting him, it was such an incredibly liberating experience. She took the bottle from her handbag. It was a very small bottle, but then it was a very expensive substance. Not to mention hard to get.

'You can't imagine how much this cost me,' she purred, unscrewing the top of the bottle and tipping a little of the clear blue gel onto her index finger. She felt the burn immediately, lively and warm and enticing. 'It's the most exclusive aphrodisiac you can buy. The most powerful, too. Now, wherever shall I put it . . . ?'

Her finger drew playful circles around her breasts, circles that then became spirals and ended at her nipples. Then she covered both her hands with the ice-blue gel and smeared it down over her belly, her thighs, larding it over her buttocks, letting it trickle down to the pink pout of her inner labia. It both burned and soothed as it trickled; stung, warmed, excited . . .

'Mmm. Feels good. Aren't you jealous, Kane? Don't you wish you could give me this much pleasure?'

Kane's eyes answered for him. There was a depth of hunger in those eyes, a ravenous need, that half-terrified Alexa even at the height of her triumphant excitement.

'Come on, Kane.' She raised the bottle to her lips and, tipping back her head, drank down the remaining contents; then wiped her gloved hand across her mouth. 'Come on . . . don't you want some too? Don't you want to know how it feels?'

He seized the empty bottle from her hand, and threw it to the floor. It bounced off the carpet, and rolled away under the chest of drawers.

'You should know by now. I don't need anything . . . but you.'

Alexa growled with delight as his lips fastened on hers, licking the last of the blue gel from her mouth, her chin, her throat. As he licked his breathing quickened, and she felt his dick harden against her belly. She had to fight the urge to respond instantly, steeling herself against the agonising impulse to weaken, to throw herself at Aidan, to tear off his clothes and pleasure him with her tongue.

She wasn't going to play the slave-girl any more. This

time, Kane was going to pleasure her.

His tongue reached her nipple, circling, sucking, lapping; intensifying the delicious burning sensation provoked by the aphrodisiac gel. Good, good, it felt so good. Alexa's head swam; this stuff was even better than she'd hoped it would be. It amplified every sense; making the scent of Aidan's cologne agonisingly potent, his touch on her nipple like the rasp of a tiger's tongue.

Somehow, afterwards she couldn't quite remember how, they ended up on the floor of the hotel room, Kane on his back on the carpet, Alexa squatting over him with her bare buttocks filling his hands and her warm, sweet, shaven pussy hovering tantalisingly over his mouth.

Should she put him out of his misery now, or tantalise him a little more? It was so difficult to hold out, the aphrodisiac had done its work so well that her whole body was buzzing with the impulse to fuck, fuck and then fuck some more.

Oh, but she had such a need for cruelty in her pleasure. There could be no satisfaction unless she made Kane feel some of the pain he had made her feel. Reaching out, she took her handbag, opened it and upended it on the carpet. There they were, the two pretty toys she'd been saving up just for him.

'Another present?' he asked her, his tongue teasing the insides of her thighs, lapping up the last trickling drops of ice-blue gel. 'What a lucky boy I am.'

'Luckier than you realise. I'm going to show you how close pleasure can be to pain.'

Before his fuddled senses, dulled by the sweet treachery

of the drug, before he had had time to work out what she meant, she took hold of Kane's shirt and tore it open. In one savage movement she exposed his smooth chest and the two pink circles of his nipples, usually flat discs but now erected by excitement into flesh-pink pearls.

'I chose these especially for you,' she breathed, echoing Kane's own words to her as she forced her pussy-lips down hard onto his greedy face. At that very same moment, she reached behind her and let go of the sharp-toothed clamps, allowing them to spring shut onto his hard and juicy nipples.

She felt his body become rigid, his back arching off the floor as the metal teeth bit deeply into his nipples, sending electric shocks of brutal sensation from the fleshy nodes to the lonely, rearing spike of his cock. When he cried out, his roar of agonised bliss was lost in the folds of her sex.

'Darling Aidan, you mustn't blame yourself for your weakness. No one could possibly resist me tonight.'

Later, she might take pity on Kane and let him sink that pretty cock into her soft, ripe honeydew. But for the moment, Alexa was more than content to enjoy the sensation of having him suck at her pussy-lips, and the knowledge of his exquisite pain.

Very early the following morning, Alexa left the hotel and drove home in her work clothes, her toys securely locked in their suitcase on the back seat.

She hummed to herself as she drove, feeling good; no, better than good. Feeling like the whole world was trembling on the tip of her tongue, suddenly expectant, fearful, obedient. Things had gone exactly as she'd planned, the balance of power shifting in a way that even Aidan Kane could surely not have anticipated.

Parking in the driveway, she slid out and stretched, throwing back her head and letting the warmth of the spring sunshine caress her face. Bliss. When Piet emerged from the house a few moments later, he found her leaning back against the car and basking catlike in the sun, eyes closed, back arched and breasts pointing jauntily skywards.

'Hello Piet,' she murmured lazily, without bothering to open her eyes.

'Alexa, thank God you're all right.'

She heard the tension in his voice, imagined how he must have paced the bedroom floor all night long, wondering what was going to happen to her. It made her feel sexier than ever, knowing how easily she'd been able to make him suffer such agonies.

'Of course I'm all right.' She opened her eyes and stretched. 'You don't look too good, though,' she commented, taking in the dark circles under his hazel-gold eyes, the dishevelled hair, the unbuttoned shirt and crumpled jeans. 'Bad night?'

Piet caught her by the shoulders and pulled her towards him.

'Don't play stupid games with me, Alexa. What happened? I've been half out of my mind . . .'

I know, thought Alexa with just the merest hint of pleasurable cruelty.

'If you like, I'll tell you all about it. I think you'll find it quite . . . exciting.'

She let her hand drop to the front of Piet's 501s. The poor

boy was only half erect, perhaps because of the sleepless night and all that worry. But she was confident she could bring him to attention with just one cool-fingered caress. Slowly and efficiently she began unbuttoning his jeans.

Right on cue, her mobile rang. She reached in through the car window for it and flicked it open.

'Yes?' Not that she needed to ask. She knew perfectly well who'd be calling her at this ungodly hour, and it wasn't Damian from the agency.

'You bitch, Alexa.'

She suppressed a smile of triumph.

'Something wrong, Aidan?' She watched the expression on Piet's face turn from agonised lust to agonised jealousy. 'Missing the taste of my pussy already?'

'I did not give you permission to leave, Alexa.'

'I wasn't under the impression I *needed* permission. Yours or anybody else's.'

Kane's voice rose to an angry growl, loud enough for Piet to hear it too.

'Get back here right now, Alexa. Or . . .'

'Or what, Aidan? What are you going to threaten me with this time?' She laughed, drunk with her own sexual power. 'Go screw yourself.'

Without bothering to switch off the mobile, she threw it through the car window onto the back seat, where it landed right on the lid of the suitcase. A fitting place for it, thought Alexa. And Kane would be able to hear everything. Every word, every groan, every sigh.

'Coming, Piet?' she enquired with a come-hither smile.

'What – where?' Piet looked at her blankly, not yet quite

grasping the rules of this new game.

'Get in, Piet. We're going for a little drive.'

He looked at her quizzically.

'And when we get there?'

'When we get there, we're going to party. What I need right now is a really good *hard* screw.'

Chapter 12

The last person Piet expected to see when he came out of a meeting at the United East Asian Bank was Rhona McFee.

He found her hanging around the front steps like an out-of-work streetwalker, the overall effect reinforced by tiger-striped trousers, a too-tight stretchy black top and a fun-fur shoulder bag in black and white Friesian print.

'Rhona. What on earth . . . ?'

She laid a hand on his arm and drew him to one side, provoking a few interested stares from grey-suited passers-by.

'Sorry to come and see you at work, but it had to be somewhere discreet . . .'

'Discreet! Rhona, this is the City of London – and you're hardly dressed to blend in, are you?'

'Can we go somewhere quiet? A café or something? There's something I need to tell you. And I don't want anyone overhearing.'

'What's this all about? I've got another meeting in half an hour.'

'Please yourself, Piet. Sod off to your meeting if you want. It's your funeral.'

Rhona looked so uncomfortable that Piet relented. He
remembered the Happy Hummous sandwich bar. No one with
taste, money or a fear of salmonella poisoning ever went
there; it ought to be safe enough.

Five minutes later, they were sitting on opposite sides of
a chipped table-top, looking at each other over giant mugs
of stewed tea.

'So?' Piet took a sip of tea and wished he hadn't. He
ladled in three sugars to take the taste away.

'I guess it's safe enough here.' Rhona glanced nervously
about her. 'This person . . . the one you've been trying to
follow . . .'

Piet fixed Rhona with a steely gaze.

'Aidan Kane? The guy you said you didn't know anything
about?'

She reddened slightly. Blushing, she looked rather girlish;
and the blush went all the way down from her cheeks to the
bouncing bombs of her breasts, trying so valiantly to explode
out of her skintight top.

'Yeah. Well, I was lying.'

'So you do know something about him? Why the hell
didn't you tell me before?'

Rhona fiddled with her bra strap.

'I was worried, wasn't I? Look, Aidan Kane's a powerful
man, you don't know how powerful. You don't fuck with a
guy like that.'

'Tell me more.' Intrigued, Piet took another sip of tea
without even wincing.

'You've heard of Omni-Eye?'

'The CCTV and security device firm?' A cold finger of

suspicion trailed its way down Piet's spine. 'What about it?'

'Kane owns it. He built it up from scratch, it's huge now.'

'Good God. I've got an Omni-Eye security system at home, and I'm pretty sure the bank has one too.'

Rhona smiled and patted his hand.

'*Everybody* has, Piet, that's the whole point. Even systems that are sold under other names are really Omni-Eye. Kane invented the industry standard.' She paused. 'You realise what I'm saying, don't you?'

Piet did.

'Bloody hell,' he whistled, more impressed than angry. And he was bloody angry. 'Kane can see everything, anything he wants . . .'

'That's right, Piet. Like it or not, there are no secrets from Aidan Kane.'

Alexa planned her next move carefully, leaving no room for error. If Kane had taught her anything, it was to be thorough, careful, meticulous.

And implacable. Kane had taught her that, too; that cruelty and rejection might play their part in stimulating pleasure. She'd torn up Kane's last summons, refused all his telephone calls, to all intents and purposes blanked him out of her life. She'd let him rage, let him think whatever he wanted to think, let him threaten to expose her to Piet; meeting every new strategy with smiling silence.

By now, she knew enough of Aidan Kane to be certain that she was tearing him apart. Driving him crazy with unsatisfied desire, pushing him close to that danger zone in which neither of them could answer for their actions.

And now, she was ready to take the next step.

It was late at night when she drove into Old Swindon, parking in the empty street outside the Arcadia Gallery. The front doors of the gallery were locked, but Alexa had done her homework. She headed round the side of the building, to a much smaller entrance which was completely invisible from the road. That was locked too, but this time Alexa had gone to the trouble of obtaining a key.

She turned it soundlessly and pushed open the door. The lights were off in the old chapel, but the tape loops were still playing, over and over again, on dozens of screens, filling the gallery with flickering, almost stroboscopic, greyish light.

Mary Pickford was still lying across the iron bedstead with her skirts over her head and the butler's dick pumping in and out of her. She would keep on screaming silently, wriggling her bare backside and being utterly astonished by it all until hell froze over. For some people, pleasure would always come as a complete surprise.

Alexa walked further in, past the five screens depicting variations on the theme of masturbation. At any other time she might have lingered and let the images excite her, but tonight she needed no artificial stimulant. She was fired-up and hungry, her body singing with erotic tension, like telephone wires stretched and buffeted by the wind.

This was as good a place as any. Standing in the middle of the annexe, she leaned back and called up into the darkness.

'Kane.'

Only silence answered.

'Kane, I know you're here. This is where you live.'

Footsteps sounded on the polished parquet. Slow, measured footsteps. Alexa turned round, very slowly, to meet the source of the sound. A figure emerged from the pool of shadow behind the life-sized waxwork of Valentino.

'Alexa. I knew you'd come to me.'

She smiled at his arrogance.

'You think I couldn't live without you?'

'Naturally.' Kane took a step forward. He was half in shadow, half in light, and the contours of his sharp-featured face were accentuated. 'A woman like you is incapable of surviving without pleasure.' He turned towards her, and his eyes glittered in the light from the video screens.

'Just one moment, Kane. There's a condition.'

'How inventive.' His voice was steady, calm, even mocking.

Alexa raised her hand. There was something dangling from her fingers, something long and sinuous and black.

'This time, *you* wear the blindfold.'

She heard his breathing falter. He froze, his eyes fixed on the black velvet blindfold. And now she knew she had him where she wanted him. She stepped forward.

'What's wrong, Kane? You're not afraid, are you?'

Kane's hand fumbled in his pocket. A second later, every screen in the gallery switched to show Alexa writhing on her bed at Boroughbridge Hall. Alexa naked. Alexa with Suki Manderley's tongue lapping at her sex. Alexa wearing the blindfold.

'Ah yes,' said Kane. 'Your blindfold. A pretty toy.'

'I'd rather see it on you, Kane.'

'Why don't you take a look at the film? I particularly like

the sequence where Suki fists you while licking out your arse.'

Alexa wasn't falling for that one. She deliberately avoided looking at the pantomime of her own sensual humiliation. Kane no longer had that kind of power over her. She held out the blindfold, trailing it over his face like a pair of soiled knickers, forcing him to breathe in the fragrance of old sweat and captive desire.

'Put it on, Aidan.'

'You're not serious.' Did she really see him flinch from the velvet as it kissed his face?

'Oh, but I am. Put it on, or I leave. Now. And I'll never come back.'

He took it from her hands, his eyes locked on hers, daring her to back down and look away. But this was one confrontation she had no intention of avoiding. She laid her hand on Kane's and raised it gently to his eyes.

'Put on the blindfold, and I'll show you pleasure like you've never believed possible.'

He hesitated. Could that really be a flicker of fear in his eyes?

'Remember Oxford? That was just the beginning.'

Kane made as though to laugh off the intensity of her words. He smiled uneasily as he tied the blindfold about his eyes.

'If that's what turns you on.'

'Oh it is,' she whispered, stroking his dark hair back from his forehead. 'And it's going to turn you on, too. Make sure you tie it good and tight, I don't want you peeking.'

'Alexa . . .' His hands hesitated on the knot of the blindfold, but she prised them gently away.

'What's the matter, Aidan? Don't you *trust* me?'

Kane had never felt the pleasure of fear quite so acutely before. One moment he was in control, the movie mogul directing Alexa in her big seduction scene; the next, he had allowed himself to be blindfolded.

And suddenly, he felt his hands jerked behind him by someone so strong that it surely couldn't be Alexa. He shouted out and struggled, but rough twine was cutting into his wrists and the next thing he knew, he was knocked to the floor, where he lay squirming like a cut worm, his wrists tied to his ankles.

'Free me! Untie me *now*!'

No one answered. In the silence he heard the soft hiss of a zip fastener sliding down, then the swish of satin sliding over nylon stockings and the sound of heavier material falling to the floor. Thoughts raced and tumbled inside his head. Alexa was wearing a suit of grey woollen gabardine, the jacket tightly fitted, the riding skirt cut close to the hips then flaring out to skim the tops of her shiny white ankle boots. He imagined her wriggling it down over her hips, then sliding down her satin petticoat, her legs shiny and smooth under pale stockings with lacy tops.

He licked his lips, nervous and yet desperately aroused, his sight gone but his remaining senses heightened beyond belief. He was certain he could smell the subtle, addictive perfume of her freshly-shaven pussy. Would she read his thoughts and answer them? Would she cut his clothes from him with a razor-sharp knife, and sit herself down on his aching, throbbing prick?

'Ah. Oh yes. Yes, *do* it to me.'

Alexa's voice was slow, heavy, laden with sex. Kane turned his head towards the sound. There was another sound. The sound of another person's breathing, deeper and hoarser than Alexa's. Jealous agony gripped at his heart and squeezed it tight. Another lover. She had another lover here, pleasuring her, taunting him . . .

'You can't do this to me!' he shouted, but the only answer was a peal of soft laughter, and something told him that she wasn't even listening to his pleas. She was far too lost in her own quest for physical satisfaction.

Was she looking at him as she fucked? He shuddered at the thought, so close to coming and yet unable to come without the touch of Alexa's cool lips on his dick. He listened, because that was the only thing that he could do. There was no escape. She had found the perfect torment, the perfect stimulant to renew his lust again and again and never let it find release.

The sounds of flesh sliding over flesh. Floorboards creaking to a quickening rhythm. He imagined the sweat dripping down, the tongues lapping, teeth biting. Breathing, hoarse and harsh and shallow.

'Fuck me! Fuck me harder. Harder, harder, *harder*.'

Alexa was almost screaming with pleasure, her voice filling the whole space around Kane, getting inside his head and taunting him. Her presence possessed him, her ecstasy drove him to distraction. He rolled about on the floor, tried to pull his wrists and ankles free, but he was trussed like a

Christmas parcel and all he could do was lie there and listen.

What was she doing? What was *he* doing to make her cry out like that? Was she kneeling on all fours on the gallery floor, taking her lover's dick up her arse? Was she squatting over him and riding him like a thoroughbred, whipping him into a shared frenzy of delirious lust?

'No. No, no, please,' he whimpered, as the ache of need turned to a raging agony of lascivious pain. His balls felt so heavy that they would burst without Alexa's kisses. His dick felt like molten lead, a fiery rod he was condemned to bear as his punishment. 'Please. Alexa, please . . .'

The sounds rose to a crescendo of agonised wailing as Alexa drained the pleasure from her silent, unseen lover. Kane imagined thighs and buttocks slamming against the floor, belly slapping against belly, Alexa's wet pussy squelching about the root of a hard, fat dick. Someone else's dick. Not Aidan Kane's.

He was forced to listen to her climax, to feel her shudders as they vibrated through the wooden floor into his body. And then everything stopped, as suddenly as it had begun.

He waited. Nothing happened for a long time. Then he heard the sounds of her dressing, the businesslike zizz of her zipper, the tap-tap-tap of her high heels on the parquet floor.

The footsteps came very close, then stopped. Then came her voice, soft and treacherous as sun-warmed honey, dripping into his ear.

'Never follow me, never watch me, never bother me again – and perhaps, just *perhaps*, I'll be back.'

Her footsteps receded, disappearing into nothingness.

Alone in his own private darkness, Aidan Kane mumbled
and sobbed with need, rubbing the base of his belly against
the floor until at last he found a kind of release. A kind of
profoundly painful ecstasy, the like of which he had never
known before.

He mumbled in his delirium, calling her name again and
again.

'Alexa, oh Alexa. You perfectly perfect slut. My darling,
consummate temptress. How adorably cruel you are . . .'

And so the rules changed, once again.

Now it was Alexa who was issuing the summonses; not
every month, for that would be to play Kane's own game,
but whenever she chose – which was not very frequently, for
she did not want Kane to imagine, even for a moment, that
she needed him the way he needed her.

As far as Piet was concerned, it was all over between
Alexa and Kane. He didn't need to know about the midnight
trysts, the cries of blissful pain that might pass between two
strangers in a hotel room. He would never understand, and
so it was simply easier not to bother telling him.

Not that Piet had any objection to other adventures, as
Alexa soon discovered.

'That was an amusing game we played with Kane,' he
commented one summer evening, as they lay entwined beside
Piet's private swimming pool. 'I enjoyed getting the better
of him.'

'Mmm,' murmured Alexa, concealing her smile by taking
a sip of red wine.

'I've decided to have the security system removed,' Piet

added casually. 'I thought it best, under the circumstances.'
He stroked Alexa's breast, round and firm under her bikini
top. 'And I don't care what Damian Goldstone says, you're
not going on any more courses. Not now I know Kane owns
Boroughbridge Hall.'

'Whatever.' Alexa slid down her bra strap, baring her
breast to Piet's caresses. 'It doesn't have to stop, you know.'

'What?'

Alexa smiled.

'The game. Why shouldn't we try it ourselves?'

Piet's eyes narrowed with interest. He rolled over on top
of Alexa's damp and yielding body.

'Tell me more.'

'Well . . .' She dotted kisses all over Piet's face, neck and
shoulders. 'Why should Aidan Kane have all the fun? We
could do the same.'

Piet grinned.

'You mean, pick someone ourselves, find out a few guilty
secrets and . . . ?'

'Yeah. Exactly. Pick a . . . victim. No, a playmate.
Someone we both find attractive. Like that junior partner at
the United East Asian Bank, the one with the dark eyes and
the beautiful body . . .'

'Or that bimbo secretary at your agency. You know,
the one with the enormous breasts. Wouldn't you just love
to . . . ?'

Alexa giggled, excited by Piet's enthusiasm.

'As a matter of fact, I would. And of course, there's always
Damian.'

'*Damian*? I thought you reckoned he was an idiot.'

'Not an idiot, he's just led rather a sheltered life.' Alexa chuckled to herself, remembering his expression that day when he'd overheard her talking dirty on the phone to Piet. 'He needs a firm hand.'

'So you think he has possibilities?' Piet's tongue circled Alexa's nipple as though it were the cherry on top of an ice-cream sundae.

'Oh yes.' Alexa lay back, relaxed and thought of sweet, sweet sex. 'He *definitely* has possibilities.'

A Message from the Publisher

Headline Liaison is a new concept in erotic fiction: a list of books designed for the reading pleasure of both men and women, to be read alone – or together with your lover. As such, we would be most interested to hear from our readers.

Did you read the book with your partner? Did it fire your imagination? Did it turn you on – or off? Did you like the story, the characters, the setting? What did you think of the cover presentation? In short, what's your opinion? If you care to offer it, please write to:

The Editor
Headline Liaison
338 Euston Road
London NW1 3BH

Or maybe you think you could do better if you wrote an erotic novel yourself. We are always on the look-out for new authors. If you'd like to try your hand at writing a book for possible inclusion in the Liaison list, here are our basic guidelines: We are looking for novels of approximately 80,000 words in which the erotic content should aim to please both men and women and should not describe illegal sexual activity (pedophilia, for example). The novel should contain sympathetic and interesting characters, pace, atmosphere and an intriguing plotline.

If you'd like to have a go, please submit to the Editor a sample of at least 10,000 words, clearly typed on one side of the paper only, together with a short resume of the storyline. Should you wish your material returned to you please include a stamped addressed envelope. If we like it sufficiently, we will offer you a contract for publication.

A Message from the Publisher

Headline Delta is a unique list of erotic fiction, covering many different styles and periods and appealing to a broad readership. As such, we would be most interested to hear from you.

Did you enjoy this book? Did it turn you on – or off? Did you like the story, the characters, the setting? What did you think of the cover presentation? How did this novel compare with others you have read? In short, what's your opinion? If you care to offer it, please write to:

The Editor
Headline Delta
338 Euston Road
London NW1 3BH

Or maybe you think you could write a better erotic novel yourself. We are always looking for new authors. If you'd like to try your hand at writing a book for possible inclusion in the Delta list, here are our basic guidelines: we are looking for novels of approximately 75,000 words whose purpose is to inspire the sexual imagination of the reader. The erotic content should not describe illegal sexual activity (pedophilia, for example). The novel should contain sympathetic and interesting characters, pace, atmosphere and an intriguing storyline.

If you would like to have a go, please submit to the Editor a sample of at least 10,000 words, clearly typed in double-lined spacing on one side of the paper only, together with a short outline of the plot. Should you wish your material returned to you, please include a stamped addressed envelope. If we like it sufficiently, we will offer you a contract for publication.